The Last of the Menu Girls

Denise Chávez

Arte Público Press
Houston
1986

This volume was made possible through a grant from the National Endowment for the Arts, a federal agency.

The paper used in this publication meets the minimum requirements of the American National Standard for Permanence of Paper for Printed Library Materials Z39.48-1984.

Cover design by Narciso Peña

First Printing, 1986
Second Printing, 1987
Third Printing, 1989
Fourth Printing, 1991

Arte Público Press
University of Houston
University Park
Houston,Texas 77004

Para mi madre, Delfina Rede Chávez, quien baila en los
  cielos y en los otros cuartos . . .
For my mother, Delfina Rede Chávez, who dances in the sky
  and in the other rooms . . .

And for Daniel
Y para Daniel

Acknowledgements

My special thanks to Rudolfo Anaya, whose guidance and support have been instrumental in seeing this collection come to life, to his wife Patricia, whose kindness is immeasurable; to Antonio Márquez, David Jones, Gene Frumkin, Keith Wilson and Barry Gaines, for their invaluable comments and encouragement. My gratitude to Tom Erhard and Erlinda Gonzales-Berry, my readers, and to Marta Field and the UNM English Department. A grateful thank you to my typists Liz Smith, Becky Smith and Queene Morrison, from Manuscripts Unlimited. Thanks also to Suzanne Jamison, whose energy inspired "Evening in Paris," and to my cousin Lydia Madrid, for her drawings which captured the magic of that story. An extra special thank you to my sisters, Margo Chávez Charles and Faride Conway, who have always supported my work. Thanks and love to Daniel Zolinsky, the Best Speller in the West—my sweet pal. Thank you all for the inspiration and gentleness you've shown me. A special, prayerful thank you to my mother, Delfina Rede Chávez, who supports me still with her enduring love. God bless all of you—the Cloyd Wembleys, Braulia and Regino Suárez, and all the Esquibel family. My gratitude to God, the Spirit of this land, all the souls who have allowed me to listen in.

D.C.

Introduction

With the publication of *The Last of the Menu Girls*, Denise
Chávez joins the ranks of writers who are rounding out the
parameters of Chicano literature. The feminine voice adds a
new vision and dimension to the literature of this community.
Clearly, a new vanguard is here, and its name is woman.

In this collection, the reader will savor the poignant experi-
ences and dreams of Rocío, a young girl whose rites of pas-
sage into womanhood give unity to the collage of stories. At
the beginning of the novel Rocío cries out against the tradi-
tional serving roles which society has prescribed for women,
and she opts for the life of the artist. By the novel's end she
has found her calling, and that is to give meaning to the emotionally turbulent lives of the people she has known. It is
Rocío's mother who wisely counsels and dares her daughter
to write the story of their lives.

Denise's novel reflects her particular sense of place, revealing the depths of the world of women and the flavor of southern New Mexico. The central metaphor of the novel is the
home. The family, the known neighborhood and the role of
women in this context are Denise's concern as a writer. Her
eye for detail is sharp; the interior monologues of her characters are revealing; and Denise's long training as a dramatist
serves her well in creating intriguing plot and dialogue. In
short, all the strengths of a writer are here.

Rocío's yearning is to write a great novel from the lives of
those people she knows best. It is the same dream Denise
Chávez has followed, challenging us to let go of familiar patterns and to enter the rich and imaginative world which she
portrays with such feeling and insight.

Rudolfo A. Anaya

Contents

The Last of the Menu Girls

The Last of the Menu Girls

NAME: Rocío Esquibel
AGE: Seventeen
PREVIOUS EXPERIENCE WITH THE SICK AND
   DYING: My Great Aunt Eutilia
PRESENT EMPLOYMENT: Work-study aide at Altavista
   Memorial

I never wanted to be a nurse. My mother's aunt died in our
house, seventy-seven years old and crying in her metal crib:
"Put a pillow on the floor. I can jump," she cried. "Go on, let
me jump. I want to get away from here, far away."

Eutilia's mattress was covered with chipped clothlike sheaves
of yellowed plastic. She wet herself, was a small child, unde-
pendable, helpless. She was an old lady with a broken hip,
dying without having gotten down from that rented bed. Her
blankets were sewn by my mother: corduroy patches, bright
yellows, blues and greens, and still she wanted to jump!

"Turn her over, turn her over, turn her, wait a minute, wait—
turn . . ."

Eutilia faced the wall. It was plastered white. The foamed,
concrete turnings of some workman's trowel revealed day-
dreams: people's faces, white clouds, phantom pianos slowly
playing half lost melodies, "Las Mañanitas," "Cielito Lindo,"
songs formulated in expectation, dissolved into confusion. Eutilia's blurred faces, far off tunes faded into the white walls, into
jagged, broken waves.

I never wanted to be a nurse, ever. All that gore and blood and
grief. I was not as squeamish as my sister Mercy, who could not

13

stand to put her hands into a sinkful of dirty dishes filled with floating food—wet bread, stringy vegetables and bits of softened meat. Still, I didn't like the touch, the smells. How could I? When I touched my mother's feet, I looked away, held my nose with one hand, the other with finger laced along her toes, pulling and popping them into place. "It really helps my arthritis, baby—you don't know. Pull my toes, I'll give you a dollar, find my girdle, and I'll give you two. Ouch. Ouch. Not so hard. There, that's good. Look at my feet. You see the veins? Look at them. Aren't they ugly? And up here, look where I had the operations . . . ugly, they stripped them and still they hurt me."

She rubbed her battered flesh wistfully, placed a delicate and lovely hand on her right thigh. Mother said proudly, truthfully, "I still have lovely thighs."

PREVIOUS EXPERIENCE WITH THE SICK AND
   DYING:　Let me think . . .

Great Aunt Eutilia came to live with us one summer and seven months later she died in my father's old study, the walls lined with books, whatever answers were there—unread.

Great Aunt Eutilia smelled like the mercilessly sick. At first, a vague, softened aroma of tiredness and spilled food. And later, the full-blown emptyings of the dying: gas, putrefaction and fetid lucidity. Her body poured out long, held-back odors. She wet her diapers and sheets and knocked over medicines and glasses of tepid water, leaving in the air an unpleasant smell.

I danced around her bed in my dreams, naked, smiling, jubilant. It was an exultant adolescent dance for my dying aunt. It was necessary, compulsive. It was a primitive dance, a full moon offering that led me slithering into her room with breasts naked and oily at thirteen . . .

No one home but me.

Led me to her room, my father's refuge, those halcyon days now that he was gone—and all that remained were dusty books, cast iron bookends, reminders of the spaces he filled. Down the steps I leaped into Eutilia's faded and foggy consciousness where I whirled and danced and sang: I am your flesh and my mother's flesh and you are . . . are . . . . Eutilia stared at me. I turned away.

I danced around Eutilia's bed. I hugged the screen door, my breasts indented in the meshed wire. In the darkness Eutilia moaned, my body wet, her body dry. Steamy we were, and full of prayers.

Could I have absolved your dying by my life? Could I have lessened your agony with my spirit-filled dance in the deep darkness? The blue fan stirred, then whipped nonstop the solid air; little razors sliced through consciousness and prodded the sick and dying woman, whose whitened eyes screeched: Ay! Ay! Let me jump, put a pillow, I want to go away . . . let me . . . let me . . .

One day while playing "Cielito Lindo" on the piano in the living room, Eutilia got up and fell to the side of the piano stool. Her foot caught on the rug, "¡Ay! ¡Ay! ¡Ay! ¡Ay! Canta y no llores . . ."

All requests were silenced. Eutilia rested in her tattered hospital gown, having shredded it to pieces. She was surrounded by little white strips of raveled cloth. Uncle Toño, her babysitter, after watching the evening news, found her naked and in a bed of cloth. She stared at the ceiling, having played the piano far into the night. She listened to sounds coming from around the back of her head. Just listened. Just looked. Just shredded. Shredded the rented gown, shredded it. When the lady of the house returned and asked how was she, meaning, does she breathe, Toño answered, "Fine."

Christ on his crucifix! He'd never gone into the room to check on her. Later, when they found her, Toño cried, his cousin laughed. They hugged each other, then cried, then laughed, then cried. Eutilia's fingers never rested. They played beautiful tunes. She was a little girl in tatters in her metal bed with sideboards that went up and down, up and down . . .

The young girls danced they played they danced they filled out forms.

PREVIOUS EMPLOYMENT: None.

There was always a first job, as there was the first summer of the very first boyfriend. That was the summer of our first swamp cooler. The heat bore down and congealed sweat. It made rivulets trace the body's meridian and, before it stopped, was wiped away, never quite dismissed.

On the tops of the neighbors' houses old swamp coolers, with their jerky grating and droning moans, strained to ease the southern implacabilities. Whrr whrr cough whrr.

Regino Suárez climbed up and down the roof, first forgetting his hammer and then the cooler filter. His boy, Eliterio, stood at the bottom of the steps that led to the sun deck and squinted dumbly at the blazing sun. For several days Regino tramped over my dark purple bedroom. I had shut the curtains to both father and son and rested in violet contemplation of my first boyfriend.

Regino stomped his way to the other side of the house where Eutilia lay in her metal crib, trying to sleep, her weary eyes uncomprehending. The noise was upsetting, she could not play. The small blue fan wheezed freshness. Regino hammered and paced then climbed down. When lunchtime came, a carload of fat daughters drove Regino and the handsome son away.

If Eutilia could have read a book, it would have been the *Bible*, or maybe her novena to the Santo Niño de Atocha, he was her boy . . .

PREVIOUS EXPERIENCE WITH THE SICK AND DYING:

This question reminds me of a story my mother told me about a very old woman, Doña Mercedes, who was dying of cancer. Doña Mercedes lived with her daughter, Corina, who was my mother's friend. The old woman lay in bed, day after day, moaning and crying softly, not actually crying out, but whimpering in a sad, hopeless way. "Don't move me," she begged when her daughter tried to change the sheets or bathe her. Every day this ordeal of maintenance became worse. It was a painful thing and full of dread for the old woman, the once fastidious and upright Doña Mercedes. She had been a lady, straight and imposing, and with a headful of rich dark hair. Her ancestors were from Spain. "You mustn't move me, Corina," Doña Mercedes pleaded, "never, please. Leave me alone, mi'jita," and so the daughter acquiesced. Cleaning around her tortured flesh and delicately wiping where they could, the two women attended to Doña Mercedes. She died in the daytime, as she had wanted.

When the young women went to lift the old lady from her death bed, they struggled to pull her from the sheets; and, when finally they turned her on her side, they saw huge gaping holes in her back where the cancer had eaten through the flesh. The sheets were stained, the bedsores lost in a red wash of bloody pus. Doña Mercedes' cancer had eaten its way through her back and onto those sheets. "Don't move me, please don't move me," she had cried.

The two young women stuffed piles of shredded disinfected rags soaked in Lysol into Doña Mercedes' chest cavity, filling it, and horrified, with cloths over their mouths, said the prayers for the dead. Everyone remembered her as tall and straight and very Spanish.

PRESENT EMPLOYMENT: Work-study aide at Altavista
Memorial Hospital

I never wanted to be a nurse. Never. The smells. The pain. What was I to do then, working in a hospital, in that place of white women, whiter men with square faces? I had no skills. Once in the seventh grade I'd gotten a penmanship award. Swirling R's in boredom, the ABC's ad infinitum. Instead of dipping chocolate cones at the Dairy Queen next door to the hospital, I found myself a frightened girl in a black skirt and white blouse standing near the stairwell to the cafeteria.

I stared up at a painting of a dark-haired woman in a stiff nurse's cap and grey tunic, tending to men in old fashioned service uniforms. There was a beauty in that woman's face whoever she was. I saw myself in her, helping all of mankind, forgetting and absolving all my own sick, my own dying, especially relatives, all of them so far away, removed. I never wanted to be like Great Aunt Eutilia, or Doña Mercedes with the holes in her back, or my mother, her scarred legs, her whitened thighs.

MR. SMITH

Mr. Smith sat at his desk surrounded by requisition forms. He looked up to me with glassy eyes like filmy paperweights.

MOTHER OF GOD, MR. SMITH WAS A WALLEYED HUNCHBACK!

"Mr. Smith, I'm Rocío Esquibel, the work-study student from the university and I was sent down here to talk to you about my job."

"Down here, down here," he laughed, as if it were a private joke. "Oh, yes, you must be the new girl. Menus," he mumbled. "Now just have a seat and we'll see what we can do. Would you like some iced tea?"

It was nine o'clock in the morning, too early for tea. "No, well, yes, that would be nice."

"It's good tea, everyone likes it. Here, I'll get you some." Mr. Smith got up, more hunchbacked than I'd imagined. He tiptoed out of the room whispering, "Tea, got to get this girl some tea."

There was a bit of the gruesome Golom in him, a bit of the twisted spider in the dark. Was I to work for this gnome? I wanted to rescue souls, not play attendant to this crippled, dried up specimen, this cartilaginous insect with his misshapen head and eyes that peered out to me like the marbled eyes of statues one sees in museums. History preserves its freaks. God, was my job to do the same? No, never!

I faced Dietary Awards, Degrees in Food Management, menus for Low Salt and Fluids; the word Jello leaped out at every turn. I touched the walls. They were moist, never having seen the light.

In my dreams, Mr. Smith was encased in green Jello; his formaldehyde breath reminded me of other smells—decaying, saddened dead things; my great aunt, biology class in high school, my friend Dolores Casaus. Each of us held a tray with a dead frog pinned in place, served to us by a tall stoop-shouldered Viking turned farmer, our biology teacher Mr. Franke, pink-eyed, half blind. Dolores and I cut into the chest cavity and explored that small universe of dead cold fibers. Dolores stopped at the frog's stomach, then squeezed out its last meal, a green mash, spinach-colored, a viscous fluid—that was all that remained in that miniaturized, unresponding organ, all that was left of potential life.

Before Eutilia died she ate a little, mostly drank juice through bent and dripping hospital straws. The straws littered the floor where she'd knocked them over in her wild frenzy to escape. "Diooooooooos," she cried in that shrill voice. "Dios mío, Diosito, por favor. Ay, I won't tell your mamá, just help me get away . . . Diosito de mi vida . . . Diosito de mi corazón . . . agua, agua . . . por favor, por favor . . ."

Mr. Smith returned with my iced tea.
"Sugar?"
Sugar, yes, sugar. Lots of it. Was I to spend all summer in this smelly cage? What was I to do? What? And for whom? I had no business here. It was summertime and my life stretched out magically in front of me: there was my boyfriend, my freedom. Senior year had been the happiest of my life; was it to change?
"Anytime you want to come down and get a glass of tea, you go right ahead. We always have it on hand. Everyone likes my tea," he said with pride.
"About the job?" I asked.
Mr. Smith handed me a pile of green forms. They were menus.
In the center of the menu was listed the day of the week, and to the left and coming down in a neat order were the three meals, breakfast, lunch and dinner. Each menu had various choices for each meal.

LUNCH:
- ☐ Salisbury Steak
- ☐ Fish sticks
- ☐ Enchiladas
- ☐ Rice almondine

- ☐ Mashed potatoes and gravy
- ☐ Macaroni and cheese
- ☐ Broccoli and onions

Drinks
- ☐ Coffee

Dessert
- ☐ Jello

☐ Tea   ☐ Carrot cake
☐ 7-Up   ☐ Ice Cream, vanilla
☐ Other

"Here you see a menu for Friday, listing the three meals. Let's take lunch. You have a choice of Salisbury steak, enchiladas, they're really good, Trini makes them, she's been working for me for twenty years. Her son George Jr. works for me, too, probably his kids one day." At this possibility, Mr. Smith laughed at himself. "Oh, and fish sticks. You a . . .?"

"Our Lady of the Holy Scapular."

"Sometimes I'll get a menu back with a thank you written on the side, 'Thanks for the liver, it was real good,' or 'I haven't had rice pudding since I was a boy.' Makes me feel good to know we've made our patients happy."

Mr. Smith paused, reflecting on the positive aspects of his job.

"Mind you, these menus are only for people on regular diets, not everybody, but a lot of people. I take care of the other special diets, that doesn't concern you. I have a girl working for me now, Arlene Rutschman. You know . . ."

My mind raced forward, backward. Arlene Rutschman, the Arlene from Holy Scapular, Arlene of the soft voice, the limp mannerisms, the plain, too goodly face, Arlene, president of Our Lady's Sodality, in her white and navy blue beanie, her bobby socks and horn-rimmed glasses, the Arlene of the school dances with her perpetual escort, Bennie Lara, the toothy better-than-no-date date, the Arlene of the high grades, the muscular, yet turned-in legs, the curly unattractive hair, *that* Arlene, the dud?

"Yes, I know her."

"Good!"

"We went to school together."

"Wonderful!"

"She works here?"

"Oh, she's a nice girl. She'll help you, show you what to do, how to distribute the menus."

"Distribute the menus?"

"Now you just sit there, drink your tea and tell me about yourself."

This was the first of many conversations with Mr. Smith, the hunchbacked dietician, a man who was never anything but kind to me.

"Hey," he said proudly, "these are my kids. Norma and Bardwell. Norma's in Junior High, majoring in boys, and Bardwell is graduating from the Military Institute."

"Bardwell. That's an unusual name," I said as I stared at a series of 5 x 7's on Mr. Smith's desk.

"Bardwell, well, that was my father's name. Bardwell B. Smith. The Bard, they called him!" At this he chuckled to himself, myopically recalling his father, tracing with his strange eyes patterns of living flesh and bone.

"He used to recite."

The children looked fairly normal. Norma was slight, with a broad toothy smile. Bardwell, or Bobby, as he was called, was not unhandsome in his uniform, if it weren't for one ragged, splayed ear that slightly cupped forward, as if listening to something.

Mr. Smith's image was nowhere in sight. "Camera shy," he said. To the right of Mr. Smith's desk hung a plastic gold framed prayer beginning with the words: "Oh Lord of Pots and Pans." To the left, near a dried out water-cooler was a sign, "Bless This Mess."

Over the weeks I began to know something of Mr. Smith's convoluted life, its anchorings. His wife and children came to life, and Mr. Smith acquired a name: Marion, and a vague disconcerting sexuality. It was upsetting for me to imagine him fathering Norma and Bardwell. I stared into the framed glossies full of disbelief. Who was Mrs. Smith? What was she like?

Eutilia never had any children. She'd been married to José Esparza, a good man, a handsome man. They ran a store in Agua Tibia. They prospered, until one day, early in the morning, about three a.m., several men from El Otro Lado called out to them in the house. "Don José, wake up! We need to buy supplies." Eutilia was afraid, said, "No, José, don't let them in." He told her, "Woman, what are we here for?" And she said, "But at this hour, José? At this hour?" Don José let them into the store. The two men came in carrying two sacks, one that was empty, and another that they said was full of money. They went through the store, picking out hats, clothing, tins of corned beef, and stuffing them into the empty sack. "So many things, José," Eutilia whispered, "*too* many things!" "Oh no," one man replied, "we have the money, don't you trust us, José?" "Cómo no, compadre," he replied easily. "We need the goods, don't be afraid, compadre." "Too many things, too many things," Eutilia sighed, huddled in the darkness in her robe. She was a small woman, with the body of a little girl. Eutilia looked at José, and it was then that they both knew. When the two men had loaded up, they turned to Don José, took out a gun, which was hidden in a sack, and said, "So sorry, compadre, but you know . . . stay there, don't follow us." Eutilia hugged the darkness, saying nothing for the longest time. José was a handsome man, but dumb.

The village children made fun of José Esparza, laughed at him and pinned notes and pieces of paper to his pants. "Tonto, tonto" and "I am a fool." He never saw these notes, wondered why they laughed.

"I've brought you a gift, a bag of rocks"; all fathers have said that to their children. Except Don José Esparza. He had no children, despite his looks. "At times a monkey can do better than a prince," la comadre Lucaya used to say to anyone who would listen.

The bodies of patients twisted and moaned and cried out, and cursed, but for the two of us in that basement world, all was quiet save for the occasional clinking of an iced tea glass and the sporadic sound of Mr. Smith clearing his throat.

"There's no hurry," Mr. Smith always said. "Now you just take your time. Always in a hurry. A young person like you."

ARLENE RUTSCHMAN

"You're so lucky that you can speak Spanish," Arlene

intoned. She stood tiptoes, held her breath, then knocked gently on the patient's door. No sound. A swifter knock. "I could never remember what a turnip was," she said.

"Whatjawant?" a voice bellowed.

"I'm the menu girl; can I take your order?"

Arlene's high tremulous little girl's voice trailed off, "Good morning, Mr. Samaniego! What'll it be? No, it's not today you leave, tomorrow, after lunch. Your wife is coming to get you. So, what'll it be for your third-to-the-last meal? Now we got poached or fried eggs. Poached. P-o-a-c-h-e-d. That's like a little hard in the middle, but a little soft on the outside. Firm. No, not like scrambled. Different. Okay, you want scrambled. Juice? We got grape or orange. You like grape? Two grape. And some coffee, black."

A tall Anglo man, gaunt and yellowed like an old newspaper, his eyes rubbed black like an old raccoon's, ranged the hallway. The man talked quietly to himself and smoked numbers of cigarettes as he weaved between attendants with half-filled urinals and lugubrious I.V.'s. He reminded me of my father's friends, angular Anglos in their late fifties, men with names like Bud or Earl, men who owned garages or steak houses, men with firm hairy arms, clear blue eyes and tattoos from the war.

"That's Mr. Ellis, 206." Arlene whispered, "jaundice."

"Oh," I said, curiously contemptuous and nervous at the same time, unhappy and reeling from the phrase, "I'm the menu girl!" How'd I ever manage to get such a dumb job? At least the Candy Stripers wore a cute uniform, and they got to do fun things like deliver flowers and candy.

"Here comes Mrs. Samaniego. The wife."

"Mr. Ellis's wife?" I said, with concern.

"No, Mr. Samaniego's wife, Donelda." Arlene pointed to a wizened and giggly old woman who was sneaking by the information desk, past the silver-haired volunteer, several squirmy grandchildren in tow. Visiting hours began at two p.m., but Donelda Samaniego had come early to beat the rush. From the hallway, Arlene and I heard loud smacks, much kidding and general merriment. The room smelled of tamales.

"Old Mr. Phillips in 304, that's the Medical Floor, he gets his cath at eleven, so don't go ask him about his menu then. It upsets his stomach."

Mrs. Daniels in 210 told Arlene weakly, "Honey, yes, you, honey, who's the other girl? Who is she? You'll just have to come back later, I don't feel good. I'm a dying woman, can't you see that?" When we came back an hour later, Mrs. Daniels was asleep, snoring loudly.

Mrs. Gustafson, a sad wet-eyed, well-dressed woman in her late sixties, dismissed us from the shade of drawn curtains as her husband, G.P. "Gus" Gustafson, the judge, took long and fitful naps only to wake up again, then go back to sleep, beginning once more his inexorable round of disappearances.

"Yesterday I weighed myself in the hall and I'm getting fat. Oh, and you're so thin."

"The hips," I said, "the hips."

"You know, you remind me of that painting," Arlene said, thoughtfully.

"Which?"

"Not which, who. The one in the stairwell. Florence Nightingale, she looks like you."

"That's who that is!"

"The eyes."

"She does?"

"The eyes."

"The eyes?"

"And the hair."

"The eyes and the hair? Maybe the hair, but not the eyes."

"Yes."

"I don't think so."

"Oh yes! Every time I look at it."

"Me?"

Arlene and I sat talking at our table in the cafeteria, that later was to become *my* table. It faced the dining room. From that vantage point I could see everything and not be seen.

We talked, two friends almost, if only she weren't so, so, little girlish with ribbons. Arlene was still dating Bennie and was majoring in either home ec or biology. They seemed the same in my mind: babies, menus and frogs. Loathsome, unpleasant things.

It was there, in the coolness of the cafeteria, in that respite from the green forms, at our special table, drinking tea, laughing with Arlene, that I, still shy, still judgmental, still wondering and still afraid, under the influence of caffeine, decided to stick it out. I would not quit the job.

"How's Mr. Prieto in 200?"

"He left yesterday, but he'll be coming back. He's dying."

"Did you see old Mr. Carter? They strapped him to the wheelchair finally."

"It was about time. He kept falling over."

"Mrs. Domínguez went to bland."

"She was doing so well."

"You think so? She couldn't hardly chew. She kept choking."

"And that grouch, what's her name, the head nurse, Stevens in 214 . . ."

"She's the head nurse? I didn't know that—god, I filled out her menu for her . . . she was sleeping and I . . . no wonder she was mad . . . how did I know she was the head nurse?"

"It's okay. She's going home or coming back, I can't remember which. Esperanza González is gonna be in charge."

"She was real mad."

"Forget it, it's okay."

"The woman will never forgive me, I'll lose my job," I sighed.

I walked home past the Dairy Queen. It took five minutes at the most. I stopped midway at the ditch's edge, where the earth rose and where there was a concrete embankment on which to sit. To some this was the quiet place, where neighborhood lovers met on summer nights to kiss, and where older couples paused between their evening walks to rest. It was also the talking place, where all the neighbor kids discussed life while eating hot fudge sundae with nuts. The bench was large; four could sit on it comfortably. It faced an open field in the middle of which stood a huge apricot tree. Lastly, the bench was a stopping place, the "throne," we called it. We took off hot shoes and dipped our cramped feet into the cool ditch water, as we sat facing the southern sun at the quiet talking place, at our thrones, not thinking anything, eyes closed, but sun. The great red velvet sun.

One night I dreamt of food, wading through hallways of food, inside some dark evil stomach. My boyfriend waved to me from the ditch's bank. I sat on the throne, ran alongside his car, a blue Ford, in which he sat, on clear plastic seat covers, with that hungry Church-of-Christ smile of his. He drove away, and when he returned, the car was small and I was too big to get inside.

Eutilia stirred. She was tired. She did not recognize anyone. I danced around the bed, crossed myself, en el nombre del padre, del hijo y del espíritu santo, crossed forehead, chin and breast, begged for forgiveness even as I danced.

And on waking, I remembered. *Nabos. Turnips.* But of course.

It seemed right to me to be working in a hospital, to be helping people, and yet: why was I only a menu girl? Once a menu was completed, another would take its place and the next day another. It was a never ending round of food and more food. I thought of Judge Gustafson.

When Arlene took a short vacation to the Luray Caverns, I became the official menu girl. That week was the happiest of my entire summer.

That week I fell in love.

ELIZABETH RAINEY

Elizabeth Rainey, Room 240, was in for a D and C. I didn't know what a D and C was, but I knew it was mysterious and to me, of course, this meant it had to do with sex. Elizabeth Rainey was propped up in bed with many pillows, a soft blue, homemade quilt at the foot of her bed. Her cheeks were flushed, her red lips quivering. She looked fragile, and yet her face betrayed a harsh indelicate bitterness. She wore a creme-colored gown on which her loose hair fell about her like a cape. She was a beautiful woman, full-bodied, with the translucent beauty certain women have in the midst of sorrow—clear and unadorned, her eyes bright with inexplicable and self-contained suffering.

She cried out to me rudely, as if I personally had offended her. "What do you want? Can't you see I want to be alone. Now close the door and go away! Go away!"

"I'm here to get your menu." I could not bring myself to say, I'm the menu girl.

"Go away, go away, I don't want anything. I don't want to eat. Close the door!"

Elizabeth Rainey pulled her face away from me and turned to the wall, and, with deep and self-punishing exasperation, grit her teeth, and from the depths of her self-loathing a small inarticulate cry escaped—"Oooooh."

I ran out, frightened by her pain, yet excited somehow. She was so beautiful and so alone. I wanted in my little girl's way to hold her, hold her tight and in my woman's way never to feel her pain, ever, whatever it was.

"Go away, go away," she said, her trembling mouth rimmed with pain, "go away!"

She didn't want to eat, told me to go away. How many people yelled to me to go away that summer, have yelled since then, countless people, of all ages, sick people, really sick people, dying people, people who were well and still rudely tied into their needs for privacy and space, affronted by these constant impositions from, of all people, the menu girl!

"Move over and move out, would you? Go away! Leave me alone!"

And yet, of everyone who told me to go away, it was this woman in her solitary anguish who touched me the most deeply. How could I, age seventeen, not knowing love, how could I presume to reach out to this young woman in her sorrow, touch her and say, "I know, I understand."

Instead, I shrank back into myself and trembled behind the door. I never went back into her room. How could I? It was too terrible a vision, for in her I saw myself, all life, all suffering. What I saw both chilled and burned me. I stood long in that darkened doorway, confused in the presence of human pain. I wanted to reach out . . . I wanted to . . . I wanted to . . . But *how*?

As long as I live I will carry Elizabeth Rainey's image with me: in a creme-colored gown she is propped up, her hair fanning pillows in a room full of deep sweet acrid and overspent flowers. Oh, I may have been that summer girl, but yes, I knew, I understood. I would have danced for her, Eutilia, had I but dared.

DOLORES CASAUS

Dolores of the frog entrails episode, who'd played my sister Ismene in the world literature class play, was now a nurse's aide on the surgical floor, changing sheets, giving enemas and taking rectal temperatures.

It was she who taught me how to take blood pressure, wrapping the cuff around the arm, counting the seconds and then multiplying beats. As a friend, she was rude, impudent, delightful; as an aide, most dedicated. One day for an experiment, with me as a guinea pig, she took the blood pressure of my right leg. That day I hobbled around the hospital, the leg cramped and weak. In high school Dolores had been my double, my confidante and the best Ouija board partner I ever had. When we set our fingers to the board, the dial raced and spun, flinging out letters—notes from the long dead, the crying out. Together we contacted la Llorona and would have unraveled *that* mystery if Sister Esperidiana hadn't caught us in the religion room during lunchtime communing with that distressed spirit who had so much to tell!

Dolores was engaged. She had a hope chest. She wasn't going to college because she had to work, and her two sisters-in-law, the Nurses González and González—Esperanza, male, and Bertha, female, were her supervisors.

As a favor to Dolores, González the Elder, Esperanza would often give her a left-over tray of "regular" food, the patient having checked out or on to other resting grounds. Usually I'd have gone home after the ritualistic glass of tea but one day, out of boredom perhaps, most likely out of curiosity, I hung around the surgical floor talking to Dolores, my only friend in all the hospital. I clung to her sense of wonder, her sense of the ludicrous, to her humor in the face of order, for even in that environment of restriction, I felt her still probing the whys and wherefores of science, looking for vestiges of irregularity with immense childlike curiosity.

The day of the left-over meal found Dolores and me in the laundry room, sandwiched between bins of feces and urine stained sheets to be laundered. There were also dripping urinals waiting to be washed. Hunched over a tray of fried chicken, mashed potatoes and gravy, lima beans and vanilla ice cream, we devoured crusty morsels of Mr. Smith's fried chicken breasts. The food was good. We fought over the ice cream. I resolved to try a few more \meals before the summer ended, perhaps in a more pleasant atmosphere.

That day, I lingered at the hospital longer than usual. I helped Dolores with Francisca Pacheco, turning the old woman on her side as we fitted the sheet on the mattress. "Cuidado, no me toquen," she cried. When Dolores took her temperature rectally, I left the room, but returned just as quickly, ashamed of my timidity. I was always the passing menu girl, too afraid to linger, too unwilling to see, too busy with summer illusions. Every day I raced to finish the daily menus, punching in my time card, greeting the beginning of what I considered to be my *real* day outside those long and smelly corridors where food and illness intermingled, leaving a sweet thick air of exasperation in my lungs. The "ooooh" of Elizabeth Rainey's anxious flesh.

The "ay ay ay" of Great Aunt Eutilia's phantom cries awaited me in my father's room. On the wall the portrait of his hero Napoleon hung, shielded by white sheets. The sun was too bright that summer for delicate fading eyes, the heat too oppressive. The blue fan raced to bring freshness to that acrid tomb full of ghosts.

I walked home slowly, not stopping at the quiet place. Compadre Regino Suárez was on the roof. The cooler leaked. Impatient with Regino and his hearty wave, his habit of never doing any job thoroughly, I remembered that I'd forgotten my daily iced tea. The sun was hot. All I wanted was to rest in the cool darkness of my purple room.

The inside of the house smelled of burnt food and lemons. My mother had left something on the stove again. To counteract the burnt smell she'd placed lemons all over the house. Lemons filled ashtrays and bowls, the lay solidly on tables and rested in hot corners. I looked in the direction of Eutilia's room. Quiet. She was sleeping. She'd been dead five years but, still, the room was hers. She was sleeping peacefully. I smelled the cleansing bitterness of lemons.

MRS. DANIELS

When I entered rooms and saw sick, dying women in their forties, I always remembered room 210, Mrs. Daniels, the mother of my cousin's future wife.

Mrs. Daniels usually lay in bed, whimpering like a little dog, moaning to her husband, who always stood nearby, holding her hand, saying softly, "Now, Martha, Martha. The little girl only wants to get your order."

"Send her away, goddammit!"

On those days that Mr. Daniels was absent, Mrs. Daniels whined for me to go away. "Leave me alone, can't you see I'm dying?" she said and looked toward the wall. She looked so pale, sick, near death to me, but somehow I knew, not really having imagined death without the dying, not having felt the outrage and loathing, I knew and saw her outbursts for what they really were: deep hurts, deep distresses. I saw her need to release them, to fling them at others, dribbling pain/anguish/abuse, trickling away those vast torrential feelings of sorrow and hate and fear, letting them fall wherever they would, on whomever they might. I was her white wall. I was her whipping girl upon whom she spilled her darkened ashes. She cried out obscenely to me, sending me reeling from her room, that room of loathing and dread. That room anxious with worms.

Who of us has not heard the angry choked words of crying people, listened, not wanting to hear, then shut our ears, said enough, I don't want to. Who has not seen the fearful tear-streamed faces, known the blank eyes and felt the holding back, and, like smiling thoughtless children, said: "I was in the next room, I couldn't help hearing, I heard, I saw, you didn't know, did you? I know."

We rolled up the pain, assigned it a shelf, placed it in the hardened place, along with a certain self-congratulatory sense of wonder at the world's unfortunates like Mrs. Daniels. We were embarrassed to be alive.

JUAN MARIA/THE NOSE

"Cómo se dice when was the last time you had a bowel movement?" Nurse Luciano asked. She was from Yonkers, a bright newlywed. Erminia, the ward secretary, a tall thin horsey woman with a postured Juárez hairdo of exaggerated sausage ringlets, replied through chapped lips, "Oh, who cares, he's sleeping."

"He's from México, huh?" Luciano said with interest.

"An illegal alien," Rosario retorted. She was Erminia's sister, the superintendent's secretary, with the look of a badly scarred bulldog. She'd stopped by to invite Erminia to join her for lunch.

"So where'd it happen?" Luciano asked.

"At the Guadalajara Bar on Main Street," Erminia answered, moistening her purple lips nervously. It was a habit of hers.

"Hey, I remember when we used to walk home from school. You remember, Rocío?" Dolores asked, "We'd try to throw each other through the swinging doors. It was real noisy in there."

"Father O'Kelley said drink was the defilement of men, the undoing of staunch, god-fearing women," I said.

"Our father has one now and then," Rosario replied, "that doesn't mean anything. It's because he was one of those aliens."

"Those kind of problems are bad around here I heard," Luciano said, "people sneaking across the border and all."

"Hell, you don't know the half of it," Nurse González said as she came up to the desk where we all stood facing the hallway. "It's an epidemic."

"I don't know, my mother always had maids, and they were all real nice except the one who stole her wedding rings. We had to track her all the way to Piedras Negras and even then she wouldn't give them up," Erminia interjected.

"Still, it doesn't seem human the way they're treated at times."

"Some of them, they ain't human."

"Still, he was drunk, he wasn't full aware."

"Full aware, my ass," retorted Esperanza angrily, "he had enough money to buy booze. If that's not aware, I don't know what aware is. Ain't my goddam fault the bastard got into a fight and someone bit his nose off. Ain't *my* fault he's here and *we* gotta take care of him. Christ! If *that* isn't aware, I don't know what aware is!"

Esperanza González, head surgical floor nurse, the short but highly respected Esperanza of no esperanzas, the Esperanza of the short-bobbed hair, the husky deferential voice, the commands, the no-nonsense orders and briskness, Esperanza the future sister-in-law of Dolores, my only friend, Esperanza the dyke, who was later killed in a car accident on the way to somewhere, said: "Now get back to work all of you, we're just here to clean up the mess."

Later when Esperanza was killed my aunt said, "How nice. In the paper they called her lover her sister. How nice!"

"Hey, Erminia, lunch?" asked Rosario, almost sheepishly. "You hungry?"

"Coming, Rosario," yelled Erminia from the back office where she was getting her purse. "Coming!"

"God, I'm starving," Rosario said, "can you hear my stomach?"

"Go check Mr. Carter's cath, Dolores, will you?" said Esperanza in a softer tone.

"Well, I don't know, I just don't know," Luciano pondered. "It doesn't seem human, does it? I mean how in the world could anyone in their right mind bite off another person's nose? How? You know it, González, you're a tough rooster. If I didn't know you so well already, you'd scare the hell out of me. How long you been a nurse?"

"Too long, Luciano. Look, I ain't a new bride, that's liable to make a person soft. Me, I just clean up the mess."

"Luciano, what you know about people could be put on the

head of a pin. You just leave these alien problems to those of us who were brought up around here and know what's going on. Me, I don't feel one bit sorry for that bastard," Esperanza said firmly. "Christ, Luciano, what do you expect, he don't speak no Engleesh!"

"His name is Juan María Mejía," I ventured.

Luciano laughed. Esperanza laughed. Dolores went off to Mrs. Carter's room, and Rosario chatted noisily with Erminia as they walked toward the cafeteria.

"Hey, Rosario," Luciano called out, "what happened to the rings?"

It was enchilada day. Trini was very busy.

Juan María the Nose was sleeping in the hallway; all the other beds were filled. His hospital gown was awry, the grey sheet folded through sleep-deadened limbs. His hands were tightly clenched. The hospital screen barely concealed his twisted private sleep of legs akimbo, moist armpits and groin. It was a sleep of sleeping off, of hard drunken wanderings, with dreams of a bar, dreams of a fight. He slept the way little boys sleep, carelessly half exposed. I stared at him.

Esperanza complained and muttered under her breath, railing at the Anglo sons of bitches and at all the lousy wetbacks, at everyone, male and female, goddamn them and their messes. Esperanza was dark and squat, pura india, tortured by her very face. Briskly, she ordered Dolores and now me about. I had graduated overnight, as if in a hazy dream, to assistant, but unofficial, ward secretary.

I stared across the hallway to Juan María the Nose. He faced the wall, a dangling I.V. at the foot of the bed. Esperanza González, R.N., looked at me.

"Well, and *who* are you?"

"I'm the menu, I mean, I *was* the menu . . ." I stammered. "I'm helping Erminia."

"So get me some cigarettes. Camels. I'll pay you tomorrow when I get paid."

Yes, it was really González, male, who ran the hospital.

Arlene returned from the Luray Caverns with a stalactite

charm bracelet for me. She announced to Mr. Smith and me that she'd gotten a job with an insurance company.

"I'll miss you, Rocío."

"Me, too, Arlene." God knows it was the truth. I'd come to depend on her, our talks over tea. No one ever complimented me like she did.

"You never get angry, do you?" she said admiringly.

"Rarely," I said. But inside, I was always angry.

"What do you want to do?"

"Want to do?"

"Yeah."

I want to be someone else, somewhere else, someone important and responsible and sexy. I want to be sexy.

"I don't know. I'm going to major in drama."

"You're sweet," she said. "Everyone likes you. It's in your nature. You're the Florence Nightingale of Altavista Memorial, that's it!"

"Oh God, Arlene, I don't want to be a nurse, *ever!* I can't take the smells. No one in our family can stand smells."

"You look like that painting. I always did think it looked like you . . ."

"You did?"

"Yeah."

"Come on, you're making me sick, Arlene."

"Everyone likes you."

"Well . . ."

"So keep in touch. I'll see you at the University."

"Home Ec?"

"Biology."

We hugged.

The weeks progressed. My hours at the hospital grew. I was allowed to check in patients, to take their blood pressures and temperatures. I flipped through the patients' charts, memorizing names, room numbers, types of diet. I fingered the doctors' reports with reverence. Perhaps someday I would begin to write in them as Erminia did: "2:15 p.m., Mrs. Daniels, pulse normal, temp normal, Dr. Blasse checked patient, treatment on schedule, medication given to quiet patient."

One day I received a call at the ward desk. It was Mr. Smith.

"Ms. Esquibel? Rocío? This is Mr. Smith, you know, down in the cafeteria."

"Yes, Mr. Smith! How are you? Is there anything I can do? Are you getting the menus okay? I'm leaving them on top of your desk."

"I've been talking to Nurse González, surgical; she says they need you there full time to fill in and could I do without you?"

"Oh, I can do both jobs; it doesn't take that long, Mr. Smith."

"No, we're going by a new system. Rather, it's the old system. The aides will take the menu orders like they used to before Arlene came. So, you come down and see me, Rocío, have a glass of iced tea. I never see you any more since you moved up in the world. Yeah, I guess you're the last of the menu girls."

The summer passed. June, July, August, my birth month. There were serious days, hurried admissions, feverish errands, quick notes jotted in the doctor's charts. I began to work Saturdays. In my eagerness to "advance," I unwittingly had created more work for myself, work I really wasn't skilled to do.

My heart reached out to every person, dragged itself through the hallways with the patients, cried when they did, laughed when they did. I had no business in the job. I was too emotional.

Now when I walked into a room I knew the patient's history, the cause of illness. I began to study individual cases with great attention, turning to a copy of *The Family Physician*, which had its place among my father's old books in his abandoned study.

Gone were the idle hours of sitting in the cafeteria, leisurely drinking iced tea, gone were the removed reflections of the outsider.

My walks home were measured, pensive. I hid in my room those long hot nights, nights full of wrestling, injured dreams. Nothing seemed enough.

Before I knew it, it was the end of August, close to that autumnal time of setting out. My new life was about to begin. I had made that awesome leap into myself that steamy summer of illness and dread—confronting at every turn, the flesh, its lingering cries.

"Ay, Ay, Ay, Ay, Canta y no llores! Porque cantando se alegran, Cielito Lindo, los corazones . . ." The little thin voice of an old woman sang from one of the back rooms. She pumped the gold pedals with fast furious and fervent feet, she smiled to the wall, its faces, she danced on the ceiling.

Let me jump.

"Goodbye, Dolores, it was fun."

"I'll miss you, Rocío! But you know, gotta save some money. I'll get back to school someday, maybe."

"What's wrong, Erminia? You mad?" I asked.

"I thought you were gonna stay and help me out here on the floor."

"Goddamn right!" complained Esperanza. "Someone told me this was your last day, so why didn't you tell me? Why'd I train you for, so you could leave us? To go to school? What for? So you can get those damned food stamps? It's a disgrace all those wetbacks and healthy college students getting our hard earned tax money. Makes me sick. Christ!" Esperanza shook her head with disgust.

"Hey, Erminia, you tell Rosario goodbye for me and Mrs. Luciano, too," I said sadly.

"Yeah, okay. They'll be here tomorrow," she answered tonelessly. I wanted to believe she was sad.

"I gotta say goodbye to Mr. Smith," I said, as I moved away.

"Make him come up and get some sun," González snickered. "Hell no, better not, he might get sunstroke and who'd fix my fried chicken?"

I climbed down the steps to the basement, past the cafeteria, past my special table, and into Mr. Smith's office, where he sat, adding numbers.

"Miss Esquibel, Rocío!"

"This is my last day, Mr. Smith. I wanted to come down and thank you.

I'm sorry about . . ."

"Oh no, it worked out all right. It's nothing."

Did I see, from the corner of my eye, a set of Friday's menus he himself was tabulating—salisbury steak, macaroni and cheese . . .

"We'll miss you, Rocío. You were an excellent menu girl."

"It's been a wonderful summer."

"Do you want some tea?"

"No, I really don't have the time."

"I'll get . . ."

"No, thank you, Mr. Smith, I *really* have to go, but thanks. It's really good tea."

I extended my hand, and for the first time, we touched. Mr. Smith's eyes seemed fogged, distracted. He stood up and hobbled closer to my side. I took his grave cold hand, shook it softly, and turned to the moist walls. When I closed the door, I saw him in front of me, framed in paper, the darkness of that quiet room. Bless this mess.

Eutilia's voice echoed in the small room. Goodbye. Goodbye. And let me jump.

I turned away from the faces, the voices, now gone: Father O'Kelley, Elizabeth Rainey, Mrs. Luciano, Arlene Rutschman, Mrs. Daniels, Juan María the Nose, Mr. Samaniego and Donelda, his wife, their grandchildren, Mr. Carter, Earl Ellis, Dolores Casaus, Erminia and her sister, the bulldog. Esperanza González, Francisca Pacheco, Elweena Twinbaum, the silver-haired volunteer whose name I'd learned the week before I left Altavista Memorial. I'd made a list on a menu of all the people I'd worked with. To remember. It seemed right.

From the distance I heard Marion Smith's high voice: "Now you come back and see us!"

Above the stairs the painting of Florence Nightingale stared solidly into weary soldiers' eyes. Her look encompassed all the great unspeakable sufferings of every war. I thought of Arlene typing insurance premiums.

Farther away, from behind and around my head, I heard the irregular but joyful strains of "Cielito Lindo" played on a phantom piano by a disembodied but now peaceful voice that sang

37

with great quivering emotion: De la sierra morena. Cielito Lindo . . . viene bajando . . .

Regino fixed the cooler. I started school. Later that year I was in a car accident. I crashed into a brick wall at the cemetery. I walked to Dolores' house, holding my bleeding face in my hands. Dolores and her father argued all the way to the hospital. I sat quietly in the back seat. It was a lovely morning. So clear. When I woke up I was on the surgical floor. Everyone knew me. I had so many flowers in the room I could hardly breathe. My older sister, Ronelia, thought I'd lost part of my nose in the accident and she returned to the cemetery to look for it. It wasn't there.

Mr. Smith came to see me once. I started to cry.

"Oh no, no, no, now don't you do that, Rocío. You want some tea?"

No one took my menu order. I guess that system had finally died out. I ate the food, whatever it was, walked the hallways in my grey hospital gown slit in the back, railed at the well-being of others, cursed myself for being so stupid. I only wanted to be taken home, down the street, past the quiet-talking place, a block away, near the Dairy Queen, to the darkness of my purple room.

It was time.

PREVIOUS EMPLOYMENT: Altavista Memorial Hospital

SUPERVISORS: Mr. Marion Smith, Dietician, and Miss Esperanza González, R.N., Surgical Floor.

DATES: June 1966 to August 1966

IN A FEW SENTENCES GIVE A BRIEF DESCRIPTION OF YOUR JOB: As Ward Secretary, I was responsible for . . . let me think . . .

Willow Game

Willow Game

I was a child before there was a South. That was before the magic of the East, the beckoning North, or the West's betrayal. For me there was simply Up the street toward the spies' house, next to Old Man W's or there was Down, past the Marking-Off Tree in the vacant lot that was the shortcut between worlds. Down was the passageway to family, the definition of small self as one of the whole, part of a past. Up was in the direction of town, flowers.

Mercy and I would scavenge the neighborhood for flowers that we would lay at Our Lady's feet during those long May Day processions of faith that we so loved. A white satin cloth would be spread in front of the altar. We children would come up one by one and place our flowers on that bridal sheet, our breathless childish fervor heightened by the mystifying scent of flowers, the vision of flowers, the flowers of our offerings. It was this beatific sense of wonder that sent us roaming the street in search of new victims, as our garden had long since been razed, emptied of all future hope.

On our block there were two flower places: Old Man W's and the Strongs. Old Man W was a Greek who worked for the city for many years and who lived with his daughter who was my older sister's friend. Mr. W always seemed eager to give us flowers; they were not as lovely or as abundant as the Strongs' flowers, yet the asking lay calmly with us at Old Man W's.

The Strongs, a misnamed brother-and-sister team who lived together in the largest, most sumptuous house on the block, were secretly referred to by my sister and me as "the spies."

A chill of dread would overtake both of us as we'd approach their mansion. We would ring the doorbell and usually the sister would answer. She was a pale woman with a braided halo of wispy white hair who always planted herself possessively in the doorway, her little girl's legs in black laced shoes holding back, sectioning off, craning her inquiry to our shaken selves with a lispy, merciless, "Yes?"

I always did the asking. In later years when the street became smaller, less foreign, and the spies had become, at the least, accepted . . . it was I who still asked questions, pleaded for flowers to Our Lady, heard the high piping voices of ecstatic children singing, "Bring flowers of the fairest, bring flowers of the rarest, from garden and woodland and hillside and dale . . . ." My refrain floated past the high white walls of the church, across the Main Street irrigation ditch and up our small street. "Our pure hearts are swelling, our glad voices telling, the praise of the loveliest Rose of the Dale . . . ."

One always came down . . .

Down consisted of all the houses past my midway vantage point, including the house across the street, occupied by a couple and their three children, who later became my charges, my baby-sitting reponsibilities, children whose names I have forgotten. This was the house where one day a used sanitary napkin was ritually burned—a warning to those future furtive random and unconcerned depositors of filth, or so this is what one read in Mr. Carter's eyes as he raked the offensive item to a pile of leaves and dramatically set fire to some nameless, faceless woman's woes. I peered from the trinity of windows cut in our wooden front door and wondered what all the commotion was about and why everyone seemed so stoically removed, embarrassed or offended. Later I would mournfully peep from the cyclopian window at the Carter's and wonder why I was there and not across the street. In my mind I floated Down, past the Marking-Off Tree with its pitted green fruit, past five or six houses, house of strangers, "los desconocidos," as my Grandmother would say, "¿Y pues, quién los parió?" I would end up at my aunt's house, return, find myself looking at our house as it was, the porch light shining, the lilies' pale patterns a diadem crowning our house, there, at night.

The walk from the beginning to the end of the street took no longer than five to ten minutes, depending on the pace and purpose of the walker. The walk was short if I was a messenger to my aunt's, or if I was meeting my father, who had recently divorced us and now called sporadically to allow us to attend to him. The pace may have been the slow, leisurely summer saunter with ice cream or the swirling dust-filled scamper of spring. Our house was situated in the middle of the block and faced a triangle of trees that became both backdrop and pivot points of this child's tale. The farthest tree, the Up Tree, was an Apricot Tree that was the property of all the neighborhood children.

The Apricot Tree lay in an empty lot near my cousin's house, the cousin who always got soap in her nose. Florence was always one of the most popular girls in school and, while I worshipped her, I was glad to have my nose and not hers. Our mothers would alternate driving us and the Sánchez boys, one of whom my father nicknamed "Priscilla" because he was always with the girls, to a small Catholic school that was our genesis. On entering Florence's house on those days when it was *her* mother's turn, I would inevitably find her bent over the bathroom basin, sneezing. She would yell out, half snottily, half snortingly, "I have soap in my nose!"

Whether the Apricot Tree really belonged to Florence wasn't clear—the tree was the neighborhood's and as such, was as familiar as our own faces, or the faces of our relatives. Her fruit, often abundant, sometimes meager, was public domain. The tree's limbs draped luxuriously across an irrigation ditch whose calm, muddy water flowed all the way from the Río Grande to our small street where it was diverted into channelways that led into the neighborhood's backyards. The fertile water deposited the future seeds of asparagus, weeds and wild flowers, then settled into tufted layers crossed by sticks and stones—hieroglyphic reminders of murky beginnings.

Along with the tree, we children drew power from the penetrating grateful wetness. In return, the tree was resplendent with offerings—there were apricots and more, there were the sturdy compartments, the chambers and tunnelways of dream, the stages of our dramas. "I'm drowning! I'm drowning!" we mocked drowning and were saved at the last moment by a friendly hand, or, "This is the ship and I am the captain!" we exulted having previously transcended death. Much time was spent at the tree, alone or with others. All of us, Priscilla, Soap-in-her-Nose, the two dark boys Up the street, my little sister and I, all of us loved the tree. We would oftentimes find ourselves slipping off from one of those choreless, shoreless days, and with a high surprised "Oh!" we would greet each other's aloneness, there at the tree that embraced us all selflessly.

On returning home we may have wandered alongside the ditch, behind the Wester's house, and near the other vacant lot which housed the second point of the triangle, the Marking-Off Tree, the likes of which may have stood at the edge of the Garden of Eden. It was dried, sad-looking. All the years of my growing up it struggled to create a life of its own. The tree passed fruit every few years or so—as old men and women struggle to empty their ravaged bowels. The grey-green balls that it brought forth we used as one uses an empty can, to kick and thrash. The tree was a reference point, offering no shade, but always meditation. It delineated the Up world from the Down. It marked off the nearest point home, without being home; it was a landmark, and as such, occupied our thoughts, not in the way the Apricot Tree did, but in a subtler, more profound way. Seeing the tree was like seeing the same viejito downtown for so long, with his bottle and his wife, and looking into his crusty white-rimmed eyes and thinking: "How much longer?" Tape appears on his neck, the voice box gargles a barking sound and the bruises seem deeper.

There, at that place of recognition and acceptance, you will see the Marking-Off Tree at the edge of my world. I sit on the front porch at twilight. The power is all about me. The great unrest twitters and swells like the erratic chords of small and large birds scaling their way home.

To our left is the Willow Tree, completing this trinity of trees. How to introduce her? I would take the light of unseen eyes and present the sister who lives in France, or her husband who died when he was but thirty. I would show you the best of friends and tell you how clear, how dear. I would recall moments of their eternal charm, their look or stance, the intrinsic quality of their bloom. You would see inside an album a black and white photograph of a man with a wide, ruddy face, in shirtsleeves, holding a plump, squinting child in front of a small tree, a tree too frail for the wild lashes, surely. On the next page an older girl passing a hand through windblown hair would look at you, you would feel her gentle beauty, love her form. Next to her a young girl stands, small eyes toward godfather, who stares at the photographer, shaded by a growing-stronger tree. Or then you would be at a birthday party, one of the guests, rimmed in zinnias, cousins surrounding, Soap-in-her-Nose, the two dark boys (younger than in story time) and the others, miniaturized versions of their future selves. Two sisters, with their arms around each other's child-delicate necks, stand out—as the warps and the twinings of the willow background confuse the boys with their whips and the girls with their fans.

In this last photograph one sees two new faces, one shy boy huddled among the girls, the other removed from all contact, sunblinded, lost in leaves.

Next to us lived the Althertons: Rob, Sandy, Ricky and Randy. The history of the house next door was wrought with struggle. Before the Althertons moved in, the Cardozas lived there, with their smiling young boys, senseless boys, demon boys. It was Emmanuel (Mannie) who punched the hole in our plastic swimming pool and Jr. who made us cry. Toward the end of the Cardoza boys' reign, Mrs. C, a small breathless bug-eyed little woman, gave birth to a girl. Mr. C's tile business failed and the family moved to Chiva Town, vacating the house to the Althertons, an alternately histrionically dry and loquacious couple with two boys. Ricky, the oldest, was a tall, tense boy who stalked the Altherton spaces with the natural grace of a wild animal, ready to spring, ears full of sound, eyes taut with anticipation. Young Randy was a plump boy-child with deep, watery eyes that clung to Mrs. Altherton's lumpish self while lean and lanky Papa A ranged the spacious lawn year round in swimming trunks in search of crab grass, weeds, any vestiges of irregularity. Lifting a handful of repugnant weed, he'd wave it in the direction of Sandy, his wife, a pigeon of a woman who cooed, "You don't say . . ."

Jack Spratt shall eat no fat, his wife shall eat no lean, and between them both, you see, they licked the platter clean.

The Altherton yard was very large, centered by a metal pole to which was attached the neighborhood's first tetherball. From our porch where my sister and I sat dressing dolls, we could hear the punch and whirr of balls, the crying and calling out. Ricky would always win, sending Randy racing inside to Mrs. A's side, at which time, having dispatched his odious brother, Ricky would beat and thrash the golden ball around in some sort of crazed and victorious adolescent dance. Randy and Mrs. A would emerge from the house and they would confer with Ricky for a time. Voices were never raised, were always hushed and calm. The two plump ones would then go off, hand in hand, leaving the lean to himself. Ricky would usually stomp away down the neighborhood, flicking off a guiltless willow limb, deleafing it in front of our watchful eyes, leaving behind his confused steps a trail of green, unblinking eyes, the leaves of our tree.

Every once in a while Randy would walk over to us as we sat dressing dolls or patting mud pies, and hesitantly, with that babyish smile of his, ask us to come play ball. We two sisters would cross the barriers of Altherton and joyfully bang the tetherball around with Randy. He played low, was predictable, unlike Ricky, who threw the ball vehemently high, confounding, always confounding. Ricky's games were over quickly, his blows firm, surprising, relentless. Ricky never played with my sister and me. He was godlike and removed, as our older sister, already sealed in some inexplicable anguish of which we children had no understanding. It was

Randy who brought us in, called out to us, permitted us to play. And when he was not there to beckon us, it was his lingering generosity and gentleness that pushed us forward into the mysterious Altherton yard, allowing us to risk fear, either of Mr. Altherton and his perennial tan, or Ricky with his senseless animal temper. Often we would find the yard free and would enjoy the tetherball without interruption, other times we would see Ricky stalk by, or hear the rustling approach of clippers, signifying Mr. Altherton's return. If we would sense the vaguest shadow of either spectre, we would run, wildly, madly, safely home, to the world of our Willow where we would huddle and hide in the shelter of green, labyrinthine rooms, abstracting ourselves from the world of Ricky's torment or Mr. Altherton's anxious wanderings.

I have spoken least of all of the Willow Tree, but in speaking of someone dead or gone, what words can reach far enough into the past to secure a vision of someone's smiling face or curious look, who can tame the restless past and show, as I have tried, black and white photographs of small children in front of a tree?

The changes of the Willow were imperceptible at first. Mr. W, the Greek, through an oversight in pronunciation, had always been Mr. V. The spies became individualized when Mr. Strong later became my substitute history teacher and caused a young student to faint. She who was afraid of blood looked up into the professor's nose and saw unmistakable flecks of red. The two dark boys grew up, became wealthy, and my cousin moved away. The irrigation ditch was eventually closed. Only the Willow remained—consoling, substantial. The days became shorter and divided the brothers while the sisters grew closer.

Ricky, now a rampaging, consumed adolescent, continued his thoughtless forays, which included absently ripping off willow limbs and discarding them on our sidewalk. "He's six years older than Randy," said my mother, that dark mother who hid in trees, "he hates his brother, he just never got over Randy's birth. You love your sister, don't you?" "Yes, mother," I would say.

47

It was not long after Ricky's emerging manhood that the Willow began to ail, even as I watched it. I knew it was hurting. The tree began to look bare. The limbs were lifeless, in anguish, and there was no discernible reason. The solid, green rooms of our child's play collapsed, the passageways became cavernous hallways, the rivers of grass dried and there was no shade. The tree was dying. My mother became concerned. I don't know what my little sister thought; she was a year younger than I. She probably thought as I did, for at that time she held me close as model and heroine, and enveloped me with her love, something Randy was never able to do for his older brother, that bewildered boy.

It wasn't until years later (although the knowledge was there, admitted, seen) that my mother told me that one day she went outside to see Ricky standing on a ladder under our Willow. He had a pair of scissors in his hands and was cutting whole branches off the tree and throwing them to one side. Mother said, "What are you doing, Ricky?" He replied, "I'm cutting the tree." "Do you realize that you're killing it?" she responded calmly. It is here that the interpretation breaks down, where the photographs fade into grey wash, and I momentarily forget what Ricky's reply was, that day, so many years ago, as the limbs of our Willow fell about him, cascading tears, willow reminders past the face of my mother, who stood solemnly and without horror.

Later, when there was no recourse but to cut down the tree, Regino Suárez, the neighborhood handyman, and his son were called in.

Regino and his son had difficulty with the tree; she refused to come out of the earth. When her roots were ripped up, there lay a cavity of dirt, an enormous aching hole, like a tooth gone, the sides impressed with myriad twistings and turnings. The trunk was moved to the side of the house, where it remained until several years ago, when it was cut up for firewood, and even then, part of the stump was left. Throughout the rest of grade school, high school, and college—until I went away, returned, went away—the Willow stump remained underneath the window of my old room.

Often I would look out and see it there, or on thoughtful walks, I would go outside near the Altherton's old house, now sealed by a tall concrete wall, and I would feel the aging hardness of the Willow's flesh.

That painful, furrowed space was left in the front yard, where once the Willow had been. It filled my eyes, my sister's eyes, my mother's eyes. The wall of trees, backdrop of the traveling me, that triangle of trees—the Apricot Tree, the Marking-Off Tree, the Willow Tree—was no longer.

One day Ricky disappeared and we were told that he'd been sent to a home for sick boys.

As children one felt dull, leaden aches that were voiceless cries and were incommunicable. The place they sprung from seemed so desolate and uninhabited and did not touch on anything tangible or transferable. To carry pain around as a child does, in that particular place, that worldless, grey corridor, and to be unable to find the syllables with which to vent one's sorrow, one's horror . . . surely this is insufferable anguish, the most insufferable. Being unable to see, yet able, willing, yet unwilling . . . to comprehend. A child's sorrow is a place that cannot be visited by others. Always the going back is solitary, and the little sisters, however much they love you, were never really very near, and the mothers, well, they stand as I said before, solemnly, without horror, removed from children by their understanding.

I am left with recollections of pain, of loss, with holes to be filled. Time, like trees, withstands the winters, bursts forth new leaves from the dried old sorrows—who knows when and why—and shelters us with the shade of later compassions, loves, although at the time the heart is seared so badly that the hope of all future flowerings is gone.

Much later, after the death of the Willow, I was walking to school when a young boy came up to me and punched me in the stomach. I doubled over, crawled back to Sister Elaine's room, unable to tell her of my recent attack, unprovoked, thoughtless, insane. What could I say to her? To my mother and father? What can I say to you? All has been told. The shreds of magic living, like the silken, green ropes of the

Willow's branches, dissolved about me, and I was beyond myself, a child no longer. I was filled with immense sadness, the burning of snow in a desert land of consistent warmth.

I walked outside and the same experience repeated itself; oh, not the same form, but yes, the attack. I was the same child, you see, mouthing pacifications, incantations . . . "Bring flowers of the fairest, bring flowers of the rarest. It's okay, from garden and woodland and hillside and dale. Our pure hearts are swelling. It's all right, our glad voices are telling, please, the praise of the loveliest rose of the dale."

Jack Spratt could eat no fat, his wife could eat no lean, and between them both, you see, they licked the platter clean . . .

My mother planted a willow several years ago, so that if you sit on the porch and face left you will see it, thriving. It's not in the same spot as its predecessor, too far right, but of course, the leveling was never done, and how was Regino to know? The Apricot Tree died, the Marking-Off Tree is fruitless now, relieved from its round of senseless birthings. This willow tree is new, with its particular joys. It stands in the center of the block . . . between.

Shooting Stars

Shooting Stars

When I was a young girl, images were conjured up in the white walls in my father's old study room. Faces leaped out from the plaster's twists and turns. These imaginings consumed the lazy summer afternoons. I was supposed to have been napping, but inevitably I wandered back to the faces in the walls, to the vast ruminations of my adolescent self.

What did it mean to be a woman? To be beautiful, complete? Was beauty a physical or a spiritual thing, was it strength of emotion, resolve, a willingness to love? What was it then, that made women lovely?

The images in the wall receded and then like bright dancing beams of light burst into my consciousness. I thought of Eloisa, Diana and Josie. One by one their faces broke out of the wall's textured surface and into my dreams to become living flesh and blood.

In my mind I was back in Texas, a place I always apologized for. It was a place removed from normal experience, the farthest spot away from my reality. As a part of that unvoiced obedience to parental rule, my sister and I spent a portion of each summer with my mother's Texas relatives.

One of our favorite pastimes was to sell wild flowers in a makeshift shop constructed by sticking clumps of stray flowers in my aunt's stone wall, with its cinderblock slots. We picked the flowers in a vacant lot sectioned off by a chain link fence that spiraled downward into an uncultivated field of wildflowers. Occasionally, the greyed and moving form of an old man materialized, alongside that of several angry dogs. Never was our flower industry totally shut down. The summer days passed this way, one upon another, in the ritual of the flower picking. No one knew of this flower industry, no one ever bought these flowers, but it mattered little to my sister and me. Each day we would set out our display, pricing and haggling between ourselves, then sitting down to wait for customers. It did not matter that our shop lay at the end of a dead-end street, or that the summer heat wilted customer and flower alike.

These days passed from the early morning obscurities of waking up, dressing, eating breakfast and wandering about the house to heightened afternoons of rummaging through my grandmother's shelves. They held warm, softened objects, handkerchiefs and embroidered limpiadores with pale stitched roses on a fading background of days: Lunes, Martes, Miércoles. In the corners, wrapped in filmy plastic bags, were peinetas still holding tufts of strong, dark hair. Later I would go through my aunt's chest of drawers. Although it was never spoken of, I knew my aunt had cancer and was dying. In her drawers were pieces of paper with obscure names, felt bookmarkers and small handbound books with either God or Daisy in the title. I found one time a collection of *Fairy Tales*, all unread, that still haunt me today. In one story, several dogs, with eyes like huge, wild saucers, guarded a magic spell-bound castle. In another a mermaid whose fins were replaced by bleeding feet learned to walk on land, beside an unfeeling lover who did not know her pain of loving.

In those days of stories, there were mudpies and one summer, an infestation of worms to be killed ingeniously. Death by stomping. Death by stoning. Death by fire. Death by insecticide. Death by scalding.

The worms oozed their way into my aunt's stone house, crawling from the marble floors onto the walls, and hung there, seeking shade in the torpid summer afternoons. Nearby, the bookshelf held *The Incredible Shrinking Man*, a book that I have regretted reading. As a child, I spent long hours imagining my disappearance in that ever fearful darkness children know so well.

In the evenings we slept outside, for it was always too hot in the house. Our adopted family consisted of my aunt, whose joys were watermelon and books, my silent and morose uncle, my two strange cousins, my grandmother, mother, Mercy and me. Each of us had our separate cot. Mine hugged the wall near the side of the house that faced the long hot highway that reached farther and deeper into Texas. It was a bit set off from the others. Lying down, I could see the low mountains in the horizon to my left and in front, the shadow of the straw roof that housed the makeshift barbecue pit that was used on fiestas, holy days. In the silent summer darkness, the imaginary aromatic memories of cabrito floated to me, along with the sound of phantom voices, haunted guitars.

As the hot, steaming nights grew longer, everyone would gravitate outside to the back of the house. Each cot would be surrounded by watermelon seeds, the moist remnants of that evening ritual. My mother and aunt sat on cots facing each other, eating gleefully and laughing about some past episode in the life of their favorite uncle, the incomparable Acorcinio, who as a drunk was prone to tears and, who sober, was something to be reckoned with. My uncle would be napping inside, face down on his single bed. My two cousins were nowhere to be found. Mercy, busy with her watermelon, dangled her legs between the metal grating of the cot's side. Curled up in my sheet, I would stare up into the sky. Somewhere far away a lone and anxious coyote called to the moon.

One day we rode into a small, nearby town, to vist relatives: a small, old lady with a fifty-year-old retarded daughter and a talkative middle-aged man whose father had once been my grandmother's beau.

It was then that I came to know Eloisa, a local girl, the daughter of a family friend. Her aunt wore men's shirts and pants and bound her breasts with rags. One day I found that Eloisa's mother and aunt (half men to me), were relatives! This made Eloisa, too, part of my mother's family. Most of them were a queer, unbalanced lot.

Eloisa was sixteen, already a woman. It was she who instigated the beginning of our many walks around the town, a place of well-kept churches, with large, wide streets and tiny, wooden shacks, like the one my mother's aunt, Eutilia, lived in. The two sisters were clear proof of little change—one spoke English and was the Postmistress of the town, the other was poor, hunchbacked, private.

Up Main Street we would go, past the record shop, with its few forty-fives of Tiny Morrie and Dion, near the five and dime, past the Paisano Hotel where the cast of *Giant* had stayed, the short but lovely Elizabeth Taylor and James Dean, who had allegedly wooed my teenage cousin, Zenaida. Up we'd go to the court house, and around the block, into familiar and dear streets. Our walks were without time or sense. They were talking walks, stopping walks. How I admired Eloisa! How grateful I was for her allowing me into her magical woman's world. Eloisa and I were bright girls, mature girls, and always trailing behind us was my little sister, Mercy.

Later, after the nightly watermelon, I would fall asleep under the stars thinking about Eloisa. She was Venus, I myself was a shooting star. The two of us were really one. We were beautiful girls, bright beautiful girls spitting out watermelon seeds. We were coyotes calling out to the moon.

That summer I carried Eloisa around with me—her image a holy card, revered, immutable, an unnamed virgin. That is, until the Jeff Chandler movie at the Pasatiempo Theatre.

Sitting in the darkness of the theatre, front row, little sister in tow, I saw, on my way to the candy counter, none other than Eloisa. She was sitting with friends. Smoke rose from their lips. My heart sank. I was sick with nicotine, faint with its smell. I wandered back to my seat. Jeff Chandler, tanned idol, a suddenly blanched earthworm. A nervous bull terrier yapped on the screen and I sank down in my seat, pretzel-like, sick to my heart. Eloisa smoked cigarettes!

When I had recovered from the shock, I stole my way back to the rear of the theatre, where Eloisa sat, chortling and braying like a rude goat. She was not alone, she was with a man, and he had his paws across her shoulder.

I crawled back to my seat again, faint with disappointment. I don't remember the rest of the movie, I barely remember

Jeff Chandler was in it.

I do remember that we didn't take many other shortcuts through the sculptured lawns of the First Presbyterian Church. Fall was coming. I was to go home to New Mexico, my father, the sun.

To me, Texas signified queer days, querulous wanderings, bloody fairy tales, hot, moon-filled nights, earthworms and unbought flowers. Texas was women to me: my fading grandmother, my aunt dying of cancer, my mother's hunchbacked aunt and Eloisa. All laughing, laughing. Summer was a yapping dog and a dream of becoming ever smaller.

When I lay in the solemn shade of my father's study, I thought of myself, of Eloisa, of all women. The thoughts swirled around like the rusty blades of our swamp cooler. Each lugubrious revolution brought freshness, change. Shifting through the many thoughts, I heard voices in the afternoon silence. Perhaps someday when I grow older, I thought, maybe then I can recollect and recount the real significance of things in a past as elusive as clouds passing . . .

Diana was another of those young women who suddenly appeared in my life. Diana was lovely and apparently guileless. She did not smoke. She did have a boyfriend. One day I spoke of saving myself for marriage, and Diana said that yes, she too, was saved.

Ruben, her boyfriend, was a childhood sweetheart. They used to play together. He was steadfast, loyal, dark like Diana, and very smart. Anyone who loved Diana must surely be smart. Diana had manners, was so nice. Sí Señora this and Sí Señora that. Nice. Nice and with the ugliest sister this side of Texas. Her sister had flat feet, spider veins, droopy nalgas and empty, lagaña-ridden eyes.

New Mexico is as unlike Texas as the moon is unlike the sun.

Diana was the personification of all that her sister was not. She was, like her namesake, the huntress in her clear, animal grace. She was simply Diana, fresh, bright-eyed, hopeful and kind. Perhaps too kind. But this weakness of her spirit did not manifest itself at first. Diana was my older sister when my older sister married and was continually birthing nieces and nephews for me. She was my confidante, someone I looked up to, respected, loved. Unlike her Texas counterpart, Diana was first and foremost: a friend who could never betray, no never. Nor could she see the possibility of betrayal. In this assumption of hers and mine lies all the tragedy of young womankind.

What was it, then, that made Diana beautiful to me, I thought as I sat in the kitchen, facing her small, strong back. Her body darted across the room to pick up a stray cup, now a plate. The steaming hot water rose and frosted the windows, fogging the view of the fields, the world beyond.

Diana's beauty came out of a certain peacefulness, not her own, but mine, that lived and breathed when I was with her. To me, the crowded dirty kitchen, the smell of warmed food, the humid moistness of frosty windows, all this was peace to me. Peace and love. That crowded kitchen, always and forever was a reminder of Diana who filled that space with her high, bright laughter.

When Diana laughed, she laughed at all life, at all dirt. Her laughter echoed through the room, and then the house. It crossed the fields and fogged all consciousness. All memory became as the water beads on the glass panes: small, wet, persistent, clinging pools.

Who was this woman? My mother's brief assistant, our solitary sister for so short a while?

Beauty is silent, does not speak. For when Diana spoke, she was not beautiful, but naive, a little girl.

In observing Diana, I observed myself. I wanted physical beauty, and yet, I wanted to speak clearly, to be understood.

Eloisa, my earlier womanly model, had walked far into the stars, and then gotten lost in the sickening odor of cigarette smoke at the back of a crowded movie theatre. Diana now, too, was lost, but in words, words, the flow and sound of words. Her music was confused, jangled, unsure. Her thoughts were half syllables, monosyllabic utterings of someone dependent upon the repetitive motions of work, the body and its order.

The faraway fields outside the northern window opened up to other views, not of the sky, but of the fecund movements of the sweet earth's turning.

Now again that laugh.

It wasn't until later that I heard again of Diana. She and Ruben were running a home cleaning service, D and R Janitorial Service. They had two sons. Ruben left her periodically to live with her former maid. One Sunday I saw her in church, mustached, wrinkled, with frightened eyes. The dog-faced sister was nearby. She was now beautiful and happily married. La Comadre Clara, Diana's mother, an old spotted monkey in ribbons, said to me, "Ay, Rocío, aquí está la Diana! Diana! You remember her?" Mother of God, Diana, the goddess, I thought, she's gone . . .

My speculations into womanhood seemed so far away from me at this point, unreachable, hopeless. The face of Diana vanished into the concrete walls.

I closed my eyes. I imagined I was on La Calle del Encuentro going past the Márquez house. In my waking life I never got inside.

Josie lived there with her mother and sister, Mary Alice. It was the same street my uncle lived on, the uncle who had a swimming pool. As a result of that, the street was revered in my mind. It was probably one of the widest in town. It was a broad, empty street that lapped into the houses of my uncle, the house of the transients (later to become the house of my cousin with the gold toothpick) and the house of the Romanos. Every day paunchy and balding Mr. Romano would dash outside in his sleeveless t-shirt and khaki shorts to get the evening paper and move the hose to the rosebushes. His was a house where tragedy lived and bloomed, like the blood red roses in the front yard. One of his children died by suicide, the other was run over by a truck. His was a house, even in those early days, that echoed pain. Across the street, the home of the druggist lay. Up from there, on the left, was the

Márquez house, a white temple of obscure shadows, a house of women.

It seems to me that as children we drove past the Márquez home either on the way to school or back. I was always filled with unwhetted curiosity about the house, its inhabitants. The front lawn was neat, sculptured. It was apparent that no one spent much time in the yard. Too public. There was also a barricaded backyard. I always tried to catch a glimpse behind curtains or beyond the painted, white brick wall. I don't remember whether I saw anything or not. Shadows of dark-haired women, perhaps, with gestures half-completed, mouths open, in half-light. It was in this state of remembrance that I saw the form of Josie's mother. Mrs. Márquez was a tensely correct and aristocratic woman who was too beautiful for her own good. She usually spoke Spanish, a sound of clipped, sexual tension with no release. Her hair was dark brown, not black, and it framed her buried, smouldering face.

And what of Mr. Márquez? Who was he? I never saw or even heard of him, and yet, someone built that dream house. Who?

Josie's sister, Mary Alice, was a little replica of Mrs. Márquez. She was my older sister's age and I was not close enough to that world of teenage concerns to be able to say that I knew her. The impression I have of her is of a lovely dark-haired girl eating a hamburger in an ad in the Bulldog annual, 1956. The dark sister is munching happily, with three or four others, one a fellow with neat, greased-back hair, while two or three girls lean on a counter, in long, pleated skirts and tight, revealing sweaters and penny loafers. Perhaps this is not the real image of the older sister, perhaps it is she that sits at the Florist's Shop, ordering a boutonniere, or maybe it is she that thumbs through the racks in the Smart Shop ad. I don't know.

While the older sister remained an indecipherable mystery to me, as did the striking mother, it was Josie, the youngest Márquez, who unwittingly found herself the subject of my insatiable gleanings and continual speculations into the mysteries of womanhood. I began my questioning with Eloisa, continued it with Diana, and was left still unsure and trembling with unanswered questions about my own uncertain womanhood when I began to study the memorable, but very short Josie Márquez.

Josie had the finely chiseled Márquez nose and full, pouty lips. Her teeth were white and even, like a small rodent's. Her eyes were the eyes of a playful and willful child. Her hands were long and slender, the nails painted red. Josie's hair was black and she wore it in trained curls around her unusually long neck that would have been prized by Japanese men who admire such anatomy. Josie had a generously full and high bust. It seemed she always managed to push it out farther and fuller than even those women with pointy, elongated breasts. She took advantage of this asset as she grew older. The necklines plunged, the dresses accented her ripe cleavage, the whiteness of her skin. From the corner of blouses and wandering into that humid maze one could discern the turning of white skin, the white meat of Josie's pale, lovely breasts.

I used to see Josie at the dancing parties held in the neighborhood by groups of older teenagers and college students who would gather to dance in someone's parents' t.v. room or vacant rental. It was here that my cousins perfected the cha-cha steps, fanning out, then touching hands, and then cha-chaing back to their sophisticated partners. It was at one of these parties that my cousin, Lorraine, only a year older than I, surpassed me, my babyness, and found her way into the light of young adulthood. It was at these parties that the embodiment of all my womanly hopes, Josie Márquez, one-two-cha-chaed her way into eternity. I stood in the darkness near the punch bowl, humming a litany of displacement to myself.

Josie was always at these parties, and either seemed to be entering or exiting. Her voice rang out greetings, burbled and chortled hellos and goodbyes. Her black spike heels clicked and turned and danced their way out the door with tall, handsome strangers, sophomores and juniors at the State University who belonged to the Newman Center and were majoring in Mechanical Engineering and who loved to dance.

Josie's closest friend was our neighbor, Barbara, who Ronelia says is doomed to her mother's face. I myself would never assign this dubious honor to her, and yet, it appears to be true. Her face, alas, was Texas stock, with a nose that would reach the horizontal boundaries of that beloved state.

Barbara was the person in those days who was always going from a tint to a rinse, from blond to brunette, from streak to different colored streak. She was a tall and gangly woman who "did the best" with what she had, and somehow managed to effect an attractiveness from her almost horsey features. Later, when she married the man of everyone's dreams, perhaps her own, his name was Derrick and he was brought up around Amarillo, a tall, handsome and rugged ex-farmer, the epitome of masculine beauty to some, to most. Barbara was the same woman who slept in her makeup, her eyeshadow and her base. This was the same woman who wore tiny, tight, curlers, a fuzzy, pink bathrobe and cried on leaving her mother's house for her own, complete with swimming pool. "Goodbye, Mama, I'll miss you."

To see Barbara and Josie was to see two disparately different body types and souls. Yet, it seemed to me that the closest womanly ties were between these two women. Both were charming, vibrant, effusive bird creatures, caught and trapped in lovely, shiny cages. They did not have the spirit of Eloisa, the gentleness of Diana, but yet, they seemed so happy to sing! Theirs was the blinding, powerful song of women, sisters!

For most of us, choice is an external sorting of the world, filled with uncertain internal emptiness. Who was I, then, to choose as model? Eloisa, Diana, Josie or Barbara? None seemed quite womanly enough. Something seemed to be lacking in each of them. The same thing that was lacking in me, whatever it was.

As I grew older, matured, I became ever more the solitary observer of my changing womanhood. I was jealous of those women who had effected the change from girlhood to woman-

hood with ease. I was at the far end of a crystal punch bowl. I heard the faraway music, saw all the colors and the lights, and yet, I was unable to join the dance.

Eloisa's gross fulfillment of the flesh, coupled with Diana's shattered dreams, somehow intertwined with Josie's pattering, pounding rhythm. I was caught in Josie's dance, and when I spun loose of all the illusionary partners, students from State, majoring in life, I felt a vague, disconcerting lack of joy. Where was the joy?

In the quiet walks, in the long summer afternoons when Diana was at the sink, laughing, telling stories in a broken language that can never be repeated. Now Josie chortles hello. Hello.

In the hazy half-sleep of my daily nap, the plaster walls revealed a new face. Behind all the work of growing up, I caught a glimpse of someone strong, full of great beauty, powerful, clear words and acts. The woman's white face was reflected in the fierce, mid-day sun, the bright intensity of loving eyes. Who was that woman?

Myself.

I thought about *loving* women. Their beauty and their doubts, their sure sweet clarity. Their unfathomable depths, their flesh and souls aligned in mystery.

I got up, looked in the mirror and thought of Ronelia, my older sister, who was always the older woman to me. It was she whom I monitored last. It was she whose life I inspected, absorbed into my own.

It was my sister's pores, her postures that were my teachers, her flesh, with and without clothes, that was my awakening, and her face that was the mirror image of my growing older. To see her, was to see my mother and my grandmother, and now myself.

I recalled Ronelia standing with her back to me, in underwear. How I marvelled at her flesh, her scars. How helpless she was, how dear! It was she who grabbed me when I was fearful that I would never be able to choose, to make up my mind. One time she and another young married cornered me, picked over me, my skin. Her friend hissed at me to tow the womanly line. "For godsakes, Rocío, stand up straight, and do *something* about your hair!" I felt hopelessly doomed to vagueness. Everything seemed undefined, my hair, my skin, my teeth, my soul. I'm incapable of making decisions, Ronelia, I thought. Leave me alone. Why are you attacking me? Go on with your babies and your fetid errands! But instead of crying out, I sat forward, bit my lip, and allowed these two young matrons to attempt a transformation of me, an indecisive girl with bumpy skin.

The charting of my sister's body was of the greatest interest to me. I saw her large, brown eyes, her sensual lips (always too big for her) soften and swell into dark beauty. At the same time, I checked myself, measuring *my* attractiveness and weighing it against my other models: Eloisa, Diana and Josie. Looking in the mirror, I saw my root beer eyes (my sister's phrase) in front of me monitoring flesh and its continuance.

I never spoke of growing old, or seeing others grow older with any sense of peace. It was a subject that was taboo, a topic like Death.

I knew that we grew older, but how could I imagine that all the bright young girls, the Jennies and the Mary Lous, the Eloisas and Dianas and the Josies, with their solid B-cups, their tangle of lovers, their popularity and their sureness, would one day become as passing shadows on the white canvases of late afternoon dreams?

The turning, plaster waves revealed my sisters, my mother, my cousins, my friends, their nude forms, half dressed, hanging out, lumpish, lovely, unaware of self, in rest rooms, in the dressing rooms, in the many stalls and the theatres of this life. I was the monitor of women's going forth. Behind the mirror, eyes half closed, I saw myself, the cloud princess.

I addressed my body, the faint incandescent loveliness of its earliest but not dearest blooming. Could I imagine the me of myself at age twenty-one and thirty-one and so on . . .

I turned the mirror to the light. The loveliness of women sprang from depthless recesses; I thought, it was a chord, a reverberation, the echo of a sound, a feeling, a twinge, and then an ache . . . .

Always there is the echo of the young girl in the oldest of women, in small wrists encased in bulky flesh, in the brightest of eyes surrounded by wrinkles. There is beauty in hands tumultuous with veins, in my grandmother's flesh that I touched as a child, flesh that did not fall, but persisted in its patterning. Her skin was oiled old cloth, with twists and folds and dark blue waves of veins on a cracked sea of tired flesh. On my dream canvas my grandmother pats her hands and says, "Someday, someday, Rocío, you'll get this way."

Women. Women with firm, sure flesh of that age in time. In dreams. Let them go. There were reflections of light, a child's imaginings at naptime, patterns on plaster walls, where shapes emerged, then receded into hazy swirls before the closing of an eye. They were clouds, soft bright hopes. Just as quickly as they were formed, they dissolved into vast pillows. Their vague outlines touched the earth and then moved on . . .

Sharp patterns on the walls and ceilings, faces in the plastered waves, all those women, all of them, they rise, then fall. Girls, girls, the bright beautiful girls, with white faces and white voices, they call out. They are shooting stars, shooting stars, spitting seeds. They are music, the echo of sound, the wind.

Somewhere very far away . . . a lone coyote calls out to the moon, her Mother.

Evening in Paris

Evening in Paris

Down the aisles of Woolworth's with my other self, Christmastime 1960, three shopping days left, a dollar for each day, and all I had was my awkward youth and one question: "What can I buy for you, Mother, this Christmas?"

The cellophane cannot conceal the rich colors of my dreams, the midnight blue bottles of *Evening in Paris*, the gift package I so long to receive myself. The deep, pungent smell is sealed in silver and blue. Twinkling stars surround me as I ponder the inevitable. But first, "Just looking."

The lady at the counter has brows like a man's, fiercer than a man's. She is someone like Mrs. Limón who lives down the street, with her brown, fish eyebrows and her fleshy, large-pored smell.

I stand while the saleslady, Mrs. Limón Jr., slides a serpentine hand along those clear compartments of ice-cold adulthood, bringing into the light pale lipsticks in pink and white, and small compact circles of Angel Face powder, translucent as the sun. No salves, ointments, colors or cremes this time— "Just looking." My hungry lips and young girl's face contemplate an unclear view of potential self.

Please hurry, I haven't time to linger. My mother and sister are somewhere in this store, this circus of objects, searching for opiates, rickrack. I am wonderstruck by the colors behind the glass, by my image in the mirror, by the smell of this blue midnight time. It is as strong as the scent of woman, faraway as Paris and full of lights.

The partitions in the case speak of care, "Now don't you

touch," the eyebrows say. Color me Rosy Red, Angel Pink, Hot Rose, Dusty Brown and Heavenly Blue. My eyes are brown. But in the mirror they are Velvet Black, Torrid Blue and Nile Green.

I take out my Christmas gift list, crossing out Father. Mother takes care of him, house shoes and a tie, signs the card "We love you, Daddy." My sister? I don't know. Mother comes first. Perfume is what I want. Limón looks at me, probably thinks to herself: "What help is there?" I wonder myself. Young make-me-beautiful girl, fill my hanging darts with the fleshed-out dreams of a dark, perfumed lady with loves. What help is there for three-dollar realities?

Mother gave me a wallet with Christ's picture on it to give to my sister. He is a Jesus anyone would love. He is so handsome with his long, curly beard and hair and deep-set eyes. He was painted by someone named Sallman, who perhaps saw him in a vision or a dream. It seems removed from me: Paris, Sallman, men become flesh. It is removed from me, my awkward limbs, uncertain dreams.

I am afraid to be seen looking at myself in the mirror, in my uniform of navy blue, with my white blouse and navy beanie, the center button of the beanie gone. Torn off. I look down to my bobby socks, the only pair I own. I wash them every morning, dry them on the heater, wear them dripping wet to school. I wore them then, in that after-school time of if only this and how to that.

I have decided to buy the gift package of *Evening In Paris Cologne and Bath Water* for my Mother. "I'll take this please," my voice falters. I don't remember how to speak, I am afraid, my clothes all wrong. Can't you cover me up? Shape my doubts, pluck the nervousness away, mask the fear and seal the lips with hope for self. Dynamite Red, of course.

The package lays heavily in my hands. I must not drop it. Oh, what a joyful treasure! This is the nicest gift I have ever given Mother. I know she'll like it, I know she will. Scent of Mother: those lilies she loves in our front yard. *Tabu* no longer her only recourse.

The Paris of Mother's dreams momentarily fused with

mine. They were one and the same, child's dreams of happiness, but more. Glory. We revel in it, rich and powdered queens, no worrying about money or any man who goes away, leaving us perfumed, alone.

I am on the edge of that vast, compartmentalized sea, looking across islands of objects, most of them man-made. I give the stranger waves of green. "Here's your change." Mother is the only one I can buy a gift for this year. I'm sorry, all of you, my friends. No one expects a gift from children, except other children. "Where's my gift?" they say, and so you look in your room, in your drawers, for something that is not used, *valuable.* I forgot about the Jesus wallet. And I can slip in a School Day's Picture. I don't know what happened to me that day. I thought I looked so good; I put the hair over my ears so they wouldn't stick out, but they did, and so did the hair.

There is a voice at the edge of this world. It is not the sour one's, she's turned away, shriveled up. The cash register has registered me. The voice calls: "Let's go, Mother's ready," and "What do you have in that package?"

Daylight darkens into dreams.

Most of the gifts under the tree are from Mother's students. We take turns passing them out—this is for you and this one and this one, too. Oh, and this is for *me!* The pile in front of Mother grows, her usual gifts are uncovered: a book of Lifesavers, Avon perfume in a white plastic vase, some green Thinking of You stationery, several cotton handkerchiefs flowered with roses, and a package of divinity, we'll all enjoy that. Most of these gifts will go into the gift box, so next year I'll have something to give my teacher. But for now, they are relegated to a temporary space on the rug, to be covered by the falling needles of our dying tree.

That particular tree lasted into February. It was with great reluctance that it was dispatched into oblivion, which in this case was the irrigation ditch behind the house. The longest tree was flocked, we did it ourselves. The flocking hung from dried bushes and clung to the yellow winter grass, all the snow that would be seen *that* year.

Summer and Dust were the only real seasons. The dry

brown grass bespoke winter and any other in-between time. Only farmers and the young, who live dependent upon change, would understand these small consistent movements toward growth. The rest of us are tucked into life's compartments, assigned worth, given shaded colors of illusion, with which to arm ourselves against changing mirrors. In days of childhood, our bright, eager faces stared from behind crystalized glass, reflected images tinted with prisms of available light, like the truncated boxes of fabricated well-being found at Woolworth's. All of us now see the edge of this material world, with its objects and playthings. But then, we were stuck! Heavenly Blue with a tinge of sweet cotton candy, little rosettes of illusion. And mine were the proudest, most sustained. They were founded upon hopes.

I recall the smell of our kitchen in those days of Christmas. There was a chicken in the oven, our Christmas "turkey." Empanadas de calabaza, indented and grooved into symmetry, lay in what might have been the "turkey tin," alongside bizcochos laid out by my Mother's holiday hands.

Most likely there was someone around to help us then: a maid from Mexico, a friend like Ninfa, who told us stories about the overly curious mouse who fell into the stew and was later eaten for his impudence. Or maybe Emilia, who showed me the round, not rectangular worlds of tortillas and how you turn-push-down-turn-keep-turning, the rolling pin, her instrument of grace. There was a familiarity of shelves and counters where one perched along blue linoleum expanses and stared into the blocked universe of Emilia's cutting board. Her squat, heavy hands, her Saviour's hands, for once she saved me from sure death on the Tilt-A-Whirl, kneaded circular balls of inanimate masa into future life. Oftentimes Emilia would lean over, and with her flour covered hands, would search the airways for her favorite station, XELO. "Ay qué lejos estoy del cielo donde he nacido," she sang, as from my Mother's room floated the sound of my favorite Christmas carol, "We Three Kings," sung so effortlessly by Perry Como.

It is enveloped in blue, this time of the past.

The shelf closest to me is one of Mother's miscellaneous shelves, her where-to-put-something-that-I-don't-know-what-to-do-with space. These four large areas contain many parts of my Mother's life. The first holds old dishes, cups and saucers, crystal plates with a thin, slightly greasy layer of moist dust, a bowl in the shape of a duck, its bright orange beak and blue eyes full of constant surprise. Near the back is a small statue of the Infant Jesus of Prague, in a long, red robe, his head awry and held in place with a wadded, previously chewed stick of old Juicy Fruit, his arms extended in benevolent greeting. This memento was the gift of some distressed Anglo woman who had spent several days with us, searching for her Filipino husband who was working in the cotton fields. She was one of the many who passed through our youthful lives, as servers or served. "Can I help you?" Mother said, and so she did, and they in turn left part of themselves with us. There was a constant stream of faces, but it is those few that I remember, like the lady with the unsteady Infant Jesus of Prague who stayed in my room and cried to herself while I slept on the couch.

The other shelves were duplicates of the first, with old dishes, broken wedding gifts, small bud vases and an occasional statuette. Amongst the clutter were other objects bespeaking personality: a twined and dried collection of palms from previous Palm Sundays, a small paper sack of cactus candy from Juárez, a stick of piloncillo, a half-empty box of Fig Newtons, a few votive candles left over from last year's luminarias, and in the corner, far from prying eyes, an ashtray filled with old cigarette butts left by my Father on his last visit. These inanimate objects assumed a banal ordinariness in full daylight, and yet their internal life danced in the darkness of significance and could never be understood by the casual observer.

Each object on those shelves had its smell and touch and taste. In those days of Sugar, it was the piloncillo that I gravitated toward, secretly chipping away rich amber edges and devouring them with delight. The cigarette butts I lifted, touched and pondered, and may have tried to smoke some in some long, solitary afternoon in the backyard, near the garbage can, in that blind space that allowed concealment, freedom.

The dishes were tokens, and each plate was embossed with streams of invisible words, known only to my Mother. How I stared into the crystaline smoothness of those inaccessible and undecipherable emotions, as a small child stands in front of the new, the novel, and as I now stand, an adult, before the sublime fluctuations of an individual heart. My Mother's heart. And so it seemed to me this Christmas that at last I had found the perfect gift for her.

When the time came around for Mother to open the dark blue gift which I had so carefully wrapped in white tissue paper, the anticipation I felt uprooted any commonplace joy I might have felt upon receiving any gifts that stood before me in "my pile."

My sister's face fell as I handed the bright white package to Mother. I quickly gave my sister a smaller unboxed gift. The red Jesus wallet. Mother had signaled Ninfa to start gathering up wrapping paper and to put the bows in a plastic bag. I asked sheepishly, "Aren't you going to open your gift?" for as far as I was concerned, there was only one. "This one, it's from me." "Yes, oh yes," she said, and stooped over to pick up several stray papers.

Later it seemed to me that perhaps Mother had thought the *Evening in Paris* had been given to her by one of her students. I even imagined that she'd been disappointed in my gift. I couldn't understand why. Maybe she actually preferred *Tabu*.

The shimmering star-filled box ended up under the tree, along with the handkerchiefs and the Lifesavers. For a long time it stayed there, unopened, unused. The Avon somehow found its way into Mother's room.

Those nights it was my custom to sit in the darkness of the living room near the tree and watch the lights. The luminarias, as seen from the windows from where I sat, hazily burned their way into the black-blue night. As usual, I felt unfulfilled, empty, without the right words, gifts, feelings for those whose lives crowded around me and who called themselves my family. How removed I felt, far away as Paris, no longer glamorous or ageless or full of illusion. The streets outside were dark and long. Much later, when I was older and found myself in Paris, it was the lost little girl who understood so much about its reality. It was the person of the inappropriate gifts who followed hunchbacked old women on winding metal stairways into a greyed, murky expanse of space with no stars. It was a Paris of balding, hennaed heads and odors of sausage exuded by men with polished, black umbrella handles that I knew, as intimately as the painted, illusionary worlds of the postcard Tour Eiffels that said, "Wish You Were Here" and "Sending Love Across the Miles."

That Paris of lights and magic exists, I have seen it, inside the haunting starless nights. And this is what I felt when I sat in the deep, embracing darkness of that special tree, the longest of all time.

Going back is going forward. It is better to give than to receive. All the familiar boring lessons are true.

The Infant Jesus of Prague with his gummed head eventually came to watch over those two ill-fated bottles of perfume. The candy changed shelves, was consumed, replaced, consumed. The wedding gifts were covered in plastic. Time was sectioned off, divided like the little boxes of painted worlds in Woolworth's. Previous intensity became a stale wash of growing up, without the standing back to choose.

I'll take this color here, that perfume there . . . that one. *Evening in Paris*. Dark blue bottle, liquid manifestation of so much hope, of long European nights, of voices mingling in the darkened streets, calling out: Remember me, remember me.

The following Christmas Mother gave *me* the Jesus wallet. She'd forgotten that the year before I'd given it to my sister, who in turn had given it to her for the gift box.

What need had Mother of perfume on those dusty playgrounds?

What need had I of wallets?

That Sallman did a good job. You know the picture, don't you? He is a Christ that anyone could love, with his long brown curls and beard. His deep-set eyes stare out.

The Closet

The Closet

I

When I close my eyes I can see Christ's eyes in the darkness. It's an early summer afternoon, and I should be sleeping. Instead, I'm standing in the silence of my mother's closet holding a luminescent sliding picture of the Shroud of Turin. One image reveals Christ as he might look fleshed out; the other shows shadows of skin pressed against white cloth. A slant of light filters through the closed door.

"It's my turn! Let me in! I want to see!" Mercy whispers impatiently from behind the door. In the half-tone darkness my eyes travel from the wedding photograph at the back of the closet to the reality of my mother's other life. Shoes crowd the floor, teacher's shoes, long comfortable plastic loafers, sandals and open-toed pumps in blue and black, the sides stretched to ease the bunions' pressure. They are the shoes of a woman with big feet, tired legs, furious bitter hopes. They are the shoes of someone who has stood all her life in line waiting for better things to come.

"Mother! Mother!" I yelled one day across the Downtown shoe store. "Is size ten too small?" She answered with an impatient pinching under-the-sweater-look reserved for nasty children who have the audacity to perform obscenities in public. She scowled across the crowded room, "No! And don't yell, your voice carries!"

Mother was married at age thirty-two to a man who bathed twice a day. Juan Luz Contreras was very clean. He was the town's best catch, a descendant of the Contreras family of west Texas. Head 'em up. Round 'em up. Ride 'em out.

Dead. Juan Luz was poisoned by an unscrupulous druggist—oh, unwittingly. He was forced to drink acid. Someone poured it down his throat, but why? He had a wife and a child but three days old. His wife was my mother. For many years I wondered who the man in the wedding photograph was. He wasn't my father. My father still lived with us at that time, but he wasn't home much. Who was the man in the photograph if he wasn't my father? Later I found out he was Juan Luz, my mother's first husband. Ronelia's father.

When my father finally left our home, it was Juan Luz's face in the crowded closet who comforted me. From all accounts he was a perfect man.

Standing in the closet I can smell mother, all of her, forty-eight years old in her flowered bathrobes and suits of gradually increasing girth. It is the soft, pungent woman smell of a fading mother of three girls, one of them the daughter of the unfortunate Juan Luz.

In the darkness there is the smell of my mother's loneliness. Next to me the portrait of my mother and Juan Luz is hidden behind piles of clothes which are crowded into the house's largest closet. All those memories are now suffocated in cloth. So whoever comes, whatever man comes, and only *one* could, he would not feel alarm. But would my father come, being gone so long?

I remember the nights my father was home, sitting in his favorite red chair, reading the evening newspaper and later telling stories to Mercy and me.

"A is for Aardvark and In the Name of the Father and The Son and Little Lulu and Iggy went to the store . . . and what did you learn today, baby?"

Sometimes, alone on the arm chair or on his lap, I recounted tales of Dick and Jane and little blond-haired Sally.

"Please, Daddy, tell me the story of the two giant brothers, Hilo and Milo."

When I open my eyes I return to the darkness of the closet. With small feet I stand on my mother's shoes. I could never fill them even if I tried.

If I didn't hold the body of Christ in my hands and if there wasn't anything to glow in the dark and then to disappear, I could still see faces in the closet and hear people talking and feel alone. I'm afraid in the middle of the day. Me, supposed to be taking a nap in August and it being the hottest month to be born in and with a crying baby sister outside the door yell-whispering, "Come on, it's *my* turn!"

And there I'd be, holding on to the brass-colored knob with one hand, and Mercy yanking with both, and the Shroud of Turin in my left hand getting crumpled and there I'd be, whispering, "Shut up, shut up! She'll hear you and so I'm looking, okay? It's *my* turn! Okay?" The boxes are open and soon scarves and hats will be all over the floor and I'll have to get a chair and put them up on the top rack and while I'm up there I'll look at the cloth flowers and feathers and I might want to play dress up with the hats.

"We'll listen to the records on the top shelf, Mercy. 'The Naughty Lady of Shady Lane' and 'Fascination.' We'll dance like we like to dance."

"We'll be floating ballerinas meeting each other halfway under the tropical bird light fixture. You can practice your diving while I count the flowers, arranging them in rows and humming. 'Let me go, let me go, let me go, lover,' while you rest from your long swim."

"It's my turn, Rocío, you get to look at the Christ eyes all the time!"

"There's no eyes. Only sockets."

"If I squint Chinesey, I can see eyes."

"Yeah?"

"So let me have the thing, it's my turn. You always look too long."

"You might get scared, baby."

"Me, no—you *promised*."

"Baby, Baby, Baby! There's no eyes, only sockets!"

"Open that door, you promised!"

"Go ahead, baby, come inside, here's the light!"

I turn the light on Christ and Juan Luz and my mother and all my dark secret young girl thoughts and face my little Sally sister with her baby limp hair.

"Go ahead Mercy Baby! Take the stupid thing. But let me look one more time." I yank on the old pink and chartreuse belt that has become my mother's light cord, and go back inside the closet for one last look. I stumble across the gift box, full of vinyl wallets and heart-shaped handkerchiefs and a plastic container of car-and-animal shaped soap. The gift box is regularly replenished by my mother's elementary school students' Christmas and birthday gifts: "Merry Christmas, love Sammy. To Teacher from Mary. You are nice, Mrs. Esquibel, I'll never forget you. Bennie Roybal. 1956."

I turn off all the lights and close the door as tight as I can. I look at the glow-in-the-dark Jesus card and slide it back and forth. The skeleton color of yellow-white bone is electrified, and I can feel and see the Christ eyes in the almost total darkness.

"So here it is, Baby! Leave me alone. I'm going to lie down on the bed and rest. Don't bother me and remember, this is the invisible line, your side, and mine. Don't cross over like you do, with those rubbery hairy spidery legs of yours. Here, see this pillow? Gosh, if we had a yardstick it would be good, but anyway, this pillow divides me from you, my side from yours, okay, Baby? I want the side by the wall and the pictures. So that when I'm drifting off to sleep, I can look at Ronelia in her wedding dress when she was seventeen years old and just married. She wore Mother's dress and Mother's veil, well, maybe not the veil, but the little plastic pill box crown with wax flowerbuds. Maybe you and I will someday wear that dress, Mercy, okay? Okay? What do you think?"

"Oh, leave me alone!" she says.

As I lay in bed, Mamá Consuelo and her husband stare at me from across the room. Their faces are superimposed on wood. It's more than a photograph. It's a carved picture of two people, one of them a stranger. I don't ever know what to call my grandfather. I never called him and he never called me. So he doesn't have a name. He's my grandfather. He was strong. He was good. He worked hard during the Depression.

He was better off than most. He died in his sleep from a bloodclot or brain hemorrhage. All I know is that he had a headache, leaped over my sleeping grandmother in the middle of the night to take an aspirin and then went back to sleep and never woke up. About Mamá Consuelo I know more.

"Oh Mercy, sleeping in the afternoons makes me tired. Without something to do or think about I'll really fall asleep. I might as well get the crown of thorns down from the crucifix and try them on."

"Are you sure, Rocío, shouldn't you leave them alone?"

Over mother's bed there's a crucifix and on the crucifix there's a crown of thorns. Real thorns, like the ones Christ was crowned with, only these are very small and they cover just the center of my head, the baby spot. It doesn't matter that they're baby-sized, because when I push them down I feel what Christ felt. Oh, they hurt, but not too much. I never pushed them down all the way. But I can imagine what they feel like. They have long waxy spikes with sharp tips. I can imagine the rest. I've been stabbed by pencils in both my palms. The one on my right looks like the Stigmata.

Naps. I hate naps because there's so much to do and think and feel, especially in August. If I have to sleep, I like it to be quick and over with before I know it, or long and happy with a visit to the Grey Room.

The Grey Room is a place I visit when I'm alone. The Grey Room was before my little-ness, before my fear of cloth shadows from clothes on chairs, and of the dark animals the shadows made.

It began when I was a little girl. I was never afraid. Every day I visited a world which the others knew nothing about. Not Ronelia, not my mother, not my father, not even Mercy.

No one knew I lived in the Grey Room or that I flew through air and time. I entered the Grey Room late at night when the house was quiet and I was alone. I'd crawl through the hall closet and into the concrete passageway that was our house's foundation. Down I would go, into the enormous basement, inching my way into the awesome darkness, alone, unhampered, guided more or less by a voice that pulled and drew me, further, further, into the concrete maze. The space became larger, a room of immense proportions, a high room, an altar room, a sanctuary where I was the only Devout. Higher, higher, I climbed, past the attic, to the labyrinth that was the Grey Room. This world was my refuge—this world unknown to all!

One day I began to live two separate lives. One magical, the other fearful. I'd wake up screaming, "The animals! The animals!" I heard the foggy mist of concerned voices. "But even you don't understand, Mercy! You always say, 'The Closet! There's nothing under our house, no rooms, no space for you to crawl through. There's no house above or underneath our house. There's no huge room without a ceiling!'

"But Mercy, I've *been* there. I've spoken to the Keeper of the Room. He's an animal and brown. He wanted to make the room smaller, but I said, no. 'There's no space for you, go away.' Now the room is white and blue and mine, alone.

"All this came to me in dreams. I felt presences and heard voices and the sound of breathing and music far away, then near. There was smoke in my room. I couldn't breathe. The animals crowded into corners. I woke up in the middle of the night trying to run away. Mother turned on the hall light to check in on me and gave me a baby aspirin. I drifted off again. 'Walking in your sleep,' mother called it.

"Mercy, would you believe me if I told you that I was born in a closet?"

"Rocío, you're crazy!"

Mother was forty years old. She'd been a widow nine years. A table was brought into the room, but the legs were removed because the doorway was too small. When I was born, Mother and I came crashing down. I shot into a closet full of shoes, old clothes. It was 4:48 a.m. on a hot August day. Ronelia hung outside the door. She was ten years old, too young to see such things.

Later, I imagined the wood, the splinters, the darkness and the shoes. And yet, on playing back the tape, Mercy, I always play back love. The things that we imagine support us never do. The world takes us quickly, handles us harshly, splinters us, casts us down and sends us forward to more pain. And yet, when I play back the tape, Mercy, I always play back love, much love.

I hear voices that say: "We are the formless who take form, briefly, in rooms, and then wander on. We are the grandmothers, aunts, sisters. We are the women who love you."

"Oh my God, Mercy, do you understand these things?"

No amount of tears will ever wash the pain or translate the joy. Over and over, it's the same, then as now. Birth and Death. There's me, in the Grey Room, or in the closet with the shoes.

"Mercy, remember the closets, remember them?"

II

The bathroom closet was full of ointments, medicines, potions to make us softer, more beautiful, less afraid. It held vials to relieve us, deceive us. It was the mysterious healing place, place of bandages, Mercurochrome and cotton balls. The center part contained the "good" towels, only used for company. They sat in their special pile, waiting for the occasional party, the welcome stranger, the annual holiday. Below this were kept the special blankets and the sheets, all folded tidily. They waited for that overnight guest or beloved family member, for nights of rearranged beds and noise and laughter. On the higher shelf were filmy containers of generic aspirin that were consumed candy-like by Mother, for headaches, backaches, heartaches. In the corner was an unused snakebite kit, with its rubber hand pump and arm tie. We fantasized this ordeal and practiced what to do if that time should ever come. The *one* time presented itself, but we were in Texas, on the way to the Big Bend National Park. The two of us had gotten off the crowded car to stretch. We heard the sound of a rattler and there we were, kitless, three hundred miles from home!

After I talked to that snake, what did you do, Mercy? I ran, wildly, madly all the way back to the car. I knew we could have died. One of us at least. It would have been me, for I was closest to the snake and saw him first. We drove on, the boy cousins up front, the girl cousins in the back. I know it would have been me.

The snakebite kit is still there, next to a greasy baby oil bottle. We never had suntan lotion until we were older, as we never had artichokes to eat, or eggplant or okra. We had summer dreams of swimming all day long, until our eyes were red, our toes and fingers pruney and our crotches white and soft and surrounded by tanned skin. Earlier we'd taken a shortcut near the Marking-Off Tree. The shortcut led to a world of water games: Splish-Splash, Tag, Dibble-Dabble. You were the swimmer, Mercy, and I the observer. In my dreams I was always just surfacing to air, having swum from an almost fatal underwater voyage. Later I stood in the darkened shade of the small blue and white bathroom, peeling off my bathing suit like a second layer of skin. My body was ice-cold and excited, slightly damp.

I stripped to summer clothes, shorts and cotton tops, and thongs. My hair was wet, in strips, my lips red, my cheeks browned, my eyes wild and smaller than normal size. My wet, slithering body found solace in cloth. I felt a great and immense hunger, as swimmers do, especially children. I took a towel from the closet, the white ones bordered in black that we were allowed to use, and saw from the corner of my eye "a miniature," placed there by my dad, who was always hiding them. I found his bottles everywhere, in his chest of drawers, under his bed. The bathroom smelled of my cool flesh, of Vicks and liquor, of old prescriptions for ever present maladies.

In the closet were remedies for women's ailments, hardened waxy suppositories, blood pressure tablets, weight pills, sulfa drugs, cough medicines, and aspirins of all sizes and shapes. There were medications for the head, the rectum, the stomach, the bladder, the eyes, the heart. The old shaving lotion was a reminder that we lived in a house of women.

An enema bag, salmon-colored and slightly cracked, the nozzle head black and foreboding, was poised and ready to be used. The last time Mother gave me an enema I was twelve, not yet a woman, but old enough to be embarrassed. I was sick, too tired to fight. Vicks and the smell of my discomfort all intermingled.

At age sixteen, I sucked in the hot, pleasant forbidden cigarette smoke and blew it out of the wire screens, hoping it would disappear. The butts were dispatched of in the usual two ways—flushed away, or wrapped in kleenex. I lit matches hoping the sulphur smell would mask my sins. But Mother knew. Mother took her aspirin not to worry about me while I smoked nude on the toilet blowing out smoke through the the meshed wire.

The bathroom was a closet. It held sexual adolescent dreams. It was full of necessities and bodily functions. Everyone hid there. Some letters from lost lovers, others, old used diaphragms.

III

I smelled Johnny. Johnny again. Johnny's blue sweat shirt jacket that he accidentally left in the living room over Christmas vacation. It was mine for three long weeks. I hung it in my closet, along with my clothes. When I closed the door I smelled Johnny, the undefinable sweetness of his young masculinity.

"Oh God, Rocío, you are so gross, you are the grossest woman I know!"

"Oh settle down, just settle down, Mercy, will you?"

The smells of the closet are lusty and broad: the smells of a young woman's body odors and special juices and the memory of slithering afterbirths. This was where I slid—into the closet full of shoes. The closet smelled of summer and long nights and red lips and drying out burnt bobby socks. I washed them every night and dried them on the floor surface. They were my one and only pair. One day they were burned beyond hope. I took them up to the attic to be hidden. My passions and fantasies were lost in time that way—stuffed into dark corners. And yet, the truth I speak is not an awkward truth. I treasured the smells and touches and the darkness of those closets. All were receptacles for a me I always wanted to be, was.

IV

The t.v. room closet was Ronelia's. Her old strapless prom dresses were there, her evening gowns of tulle, with their spaghetti straps. The closet was immense and covered the entire side of the wall. It was built by Regino Suárez. The wooden doors never opened without a struggle but got stuck midway, so that you had to push one way and then the other to get inside. In this closet were stored long dresses, costumes and party shawls, with Mother's notations, "Summer Long. Ronelia's Party. Wedding Dress, Nieves'." Alongside were her initials and the date. "Ronelia FHA Queen, 1955, Yellow Tulle, N.E."

The long cardboard boxes were crammed onto the top shelf, below them in pink and blue clothing bags were the furs, the beaver Tío Frutoso trapped himself, the suede with the fur neck piece, the imitation beige coat Mercy wore, and Mamá Consuelo's muff. The closet smelled of old petticoats and musty fur. Its contents included two wedding dresses, a new one and an old one. The new one Mother picked up at a sale for five dollars. The old one she wore when she married Juan Luz. Ronelia and Mercy later wore that dress, but at that time it was carefully sealed in plastic at the very bottom of the top shelf. Anything to do with him—photographs, articles of clothing, papers—were sacred and off-limits. To me, they were the Ark of the Covenant—deep and full of mysterious untouchability. I was ignorant of the past and the relationship of my mother to this man, long since dead.

Children assign mystery to small objects and create whole worlds from lost objects, pieces of cloth. This closet, then, was a glistening world of dances and proms and handsome dates. It was Ronelia's wedding at the age when most of us are still children. The closet meant dancing life to me. It contained my Zandunga costume, the dress I wore when I danced with Mercy as my "male" partner for bazaars and fiestas.

"Ay Zandunga, Zandunga, mamá, por dios . . . Ay Zandunga . . . Zandunga . . ."

This closet was Nieves at her best, her finest, and Mercy in imitation beige fur with a silk lining. The closet held two brides, one eternally wedded, the other, husbandless. This closet was time and fantasy and dreams—and it was Regino's—ill made.

V

The living room closet held the house umbrella in rainbow colors. For many years there was but this one umbrella, large, sturdy, friendly. It came out late summer afternoons when we played outside in the rain. It welcomed and dispatched guests, friends who had come to visit. It protected us in early fall rain storms. It shielded us in the early evening times when the fierce wildness of the unleashed summer tensions rose and fell. This closet was rain, the hope of rain. To desert souls, rain is the blessed sex of God. It cleanses and refreshes. It is still the best mother, the finest lover.

The rainbow umbrella emerged, unhooked from its long nail and was opened outside. It dried on the porch, each time a little greyer. One day it was replaced in black, by one of its funereal sisters.

This closet was the "guest" closet. It held all coats except Johnny's, which had found a dearer resting place. The overflowing "good" clothes, from the fancy dress coat closet, were placed there too. In it Christmas and birthday gifts were hidden along with the gift box. Later, paper bags full of rummage and used clothing were placed inside, on their way south. This closet was a clearinghouse—the "out-going" closet, the last stop before dispersal—to needy families, young marrieds, senior citizens who used the hand-sewn lap rugs Nieves made. It was a closet full of seasonal smells: summer rain, dark winter clothes, the faint odor of Avon perfume like dried, autumn flowers, the spring smell of soap and freshness. The closet smelled of luggage and time, of faded newspapers and old passports. Behind the door were dated check stubs and unused prayer books. The door smelled too, of wood and fingerprints. The ceiling had a trap door that led to the Grey Room. This closet was but another valve leading to the many chambers of the house's heart—where inside, beat my other life.

VI

Nieves' closet was her life, her artery of hope. Those corners were hers, unviolated. In the back, on the right, behind her clothes, was her wedding photograph. She and Juan Luz, both slim, with bright, serious faces stared out to the photographer. Behind them, leading to vast spacious rooms, was a stairway, a mirror on each side. From one wall hung the lasso, symbol of marriage. Nieves clutched a white glove in her left hand, her right arm was at a ninety degree angle. Nieves stood next to Juan Luz and both of them faced right. Her hair was short, in the style of the twenties, with soft loose curls, not as she later wore it, in a bun, austere. Juan Luz was handsome, with a full head of hair that on second glance seemed subject to thinning, if not local baldness. His hand was tightly clenched, as hers was relaxed. They gazed forward, loving, bright-eyed, with hand-painted pink cheeks. They were sealed in time—a photograph on their happiest day.

One year later, Juan Luz was dead, Nieves was a widow, Ronelia was born, and Mercy and I were still in limbo.

Moving back and up, Nieves' world was full of old records, "The Singing Nun," Augustín Lara, mementos of her teaching days, her work with children. Hers was a closet packed with scarves, new shoes, old photograph albums, a chipped statue of San Martín de Porres, tapes of the Living Bible and charismatic church revivals, as well as home movies of us as children standing by the Willow Tree.

The closet floor is strewn with paper, boxes. When Mercy and I stand in there, with the Christ eyes, we have to be careful.

"Leave me alone! It's my turn!"

"Give me the Christ eyes, Rocío!"

"Oh, go lay down, Baby."

"Don't pull that knob, Mother's gonna find out and get mad. You made me knock something over."

"Okay, okay, let me find the cord. There, see. That didn't take so long. Hey, Mercy, if you crouch down like this, it's better. That way, you feel darker."

I crouch in the closet wanting to know what it is like to feel crucified, to carry the sins of the world. I feel as if I'd already earned my crown of thorns. I imagine the splinters, the wood.

Each step into a closet was a step forward into that other world, the world of concrete corridors, the endless labyrinths, a soundless foray into the maze of faceless forms, living spirits. Up there, down there, in there, they were all the same, they lead into the heart and spirit of the house. When the spirit was sick, the nocturnal journey was long, the gasping for air at the bottom of an endless summer pool. When the spirit was pure, the long rope flew down from the sky and I was beamed up on an umbilical cord of light. I flew beyond the Grey Room into the Blue Room and further up, into the great vast No Room of the living sky. Up beyond worlds, I flew into a universe of change, to the No Place of dreamers who do not dream.

"And *how* did it happen, Rocío?" I wanted Mercy to say when I told her about the Grey Room.

"Do you think it has something to do with seeing the house's bones, I mean, its skeleton? The wood, the house frame, the concrete slabs?"

"Maybe it had something to do with seeing the sliced away mountain," I said. "Remember that mountain? All my life I thought mountains were soft inside."

"You're kidding!"

"Seeing that mountain changed my life! It was one of the five most important things that ever happened to me; the discovery of perspective in the fourth grade was three."

"What are two, four and five, Rocío?"

"I can't tell you that, Mercy."

"Tell me, tell me," she begged.

"God bless, do I have to tell you *everything*?"

"Look, I'll tell you about the Grey Room. Will you be quiet, then?" I'm in the hallway closet. I see Grandpa's death mask wrapped in white satin. I see the box of paper dolls we got on Christmas. I see your crown from elementary school, when you were Bazaar Queen. Why did you cry? I wouldn't have cried, but then I wasn't Queen. I move aside the belt cord from Mother's green bathrobe. I uncover the box of Christmas cards. I move the old rubber rain shoes and plastic rain coats. I make room for myself and step inside. I glide past everybody. I am faraway now past the color and the noise, past the cloth shadows. I am past everyone. Alone. Alone without noise. I don't need to turn on the light.

"Oh, but Rocío, aren't you afraid of the dark?" Mercy said at last, trying on the crown of thorns and then putting them on her side of the bed. "Aren't you afraid of the Christ eyes?"

"Not of the Christ eyes," I said, "but the brown animals scare me and I don't want to be afraid."

"Tell me about the Blue Room," she said, after a long pause. "It sounds *so* beautiful."

"It is," I said, lying down to rest on the bed, not bothering to tell her she was on my side again. "It's a beautiful enormous room and it's blue. But you know, the other day I went in there and it was all white and the floor was like dry ice."

"You mean it changes?" Mercy said with surprise. "Tell me about it before it changed," she said, drowsily.

"The Blue Room is my favorite room. It's the most magnificent, incredible room you'd ever hope to see, Mercy. It has a round ceiling that goes up forever. It's so big that I have to fly back and forth to get around. It's a beautiful room and it's mine. It's all mine!"

"Golly," Mercy said, yawning.

"Watch it! You almost made me turn over on the thorns. Put them up, would you?"

"Rocío, Rocío, if that's *your* room, *what's mine?*"

"I don't know, Mercy, everybody has their *own* rooms, their *own* house."

"They do?" she said with a faraway voice.

"Gaaa, Mercy, do I have to tell you *everything?*"

Space Is a Solid

Space Is a Solid

I
Kari Lee

"Space is a solid." Miss Esquibel explained this to us at the beginning of Drama Appreciation III class, but I'm not sure what she meant. Miss Esquibel told us to stand in the middle of the room, all of us kids, and "Pretend you are a molecule." Arlin was cutting up and Miss E said, "Cut it out, just cut it. If you want to squirm, wait till you're a worm." Everybody laughed, including me, even though I'm not sure what she meant by that. Anyway, Arlin was cutting up. Now, that's pretty crazy 'cause he doesn't have any arms. All he has are these little stumps which stick out like the gills of a fish. When he gets excited, they flap up and down, up and down, like wings. My friend Deanna Werner has wings too, but they're on her back. I call her The Chicken 'cause she's so skinny. When she has on a bathing suit, she makes her wings go pwaakk, up and down!

Arlin doesn't care about anything but mean boy things, like rough-housing and saying hell and damn. He'll start squawking and flapping around the room, bumping into people and Miss E will say, "Good, Arlin, good! Molecules are like that, they pop and hop!" Everyone laughs but I think he's showing off because he doesn't have arms.

Mama told me, "You mean Arlin Threadgill is in your Drama Appreciation III class, why for land's sakes, Kari Lee, he's a crippled boy! His mama was one of those that took that drug . . . Thalitomite, I think that's what they call it, causing that poor boy that horrible disfigurement for the rest of his born life. God almighty, but ain't I glad you got no stumps like that, Kari Lee Wembley. No Wembley as far as I can recollect had no disfigurement like that. And it was all on account of that Thalitomite! Drugs are dangerous, Kari Lee, look at your father's aunt, May Ethel, well, she started on some fancy prescribed drugs for her sciatica and wouldn't you know it, but she started growing hair on her face like a man! No sir, Kari Lee, no Wembley can trace their disfigurements to drugs but your Aunt May Ethel, and she was unsuspecting. Well, she stopped those drugs right then and there and endured her pain just like all the Wembleys done. Ain't right to pump your body with any enzodimes or mites, no thank you ma'am. Listen to me, Kari Lee, now if God wants to send down his wrath on you, that's another thing altogether, why, he'll do it, now just don't you go pushing him."

If Mama stood in the middle of a room, she'd be a talking molecule. I was thinking about that when Miss E turned to me and said, "Kari Lee, what are you thinking?"

"Oh, I don't know."

"Quick, tell me, don't stop to think, Kari Lee. You're a molecule, remember."

"I am?" I said, surprised.

"What does a molecule think?"

"What does a molecule think? Oh, about other molecules, I guess, Miss E. Arlin! Don't you be whapping me with those chicken wings of yours," I almost said, but I stopped in time, and said, "Molecules don't think at all, Miss E, they just move."

"Like responding to stimuli," Arlin said.

"Good, Arlin, good!" Miss Michaelson said excitedly. She's the other Drama Appreciation III teacher, Miss E's boss, kinda.

"So molecules don't talk?" questioned Miss E. She was wearing a real neat velour top. She is so pretty and so friendly and so nice and so funny! Everybody likes her except Arlin, and well, he's a pill!

Mama says that sometimes people are pills, and it's because they aren't normal, haven't got normal feelings and such, they're disfigured, and all. They call attention to themselves just like Arlin. They prance and dance around just like little circus horses, showing how much they can do. Mama says, "I don't know what's wrong with Mrs. Threadgill, showing off Arlin all over town like he was normal. No, Kari Lee, it ain't decent and all account of that Thalitomite!"

Me, I won't have nothing to do with that Arlin Threadgill, and it's not because he's a cripple. Arlin smells!

Arlin is a talking molecule and I'm a quiet molecule. Most of us molecules are quiet. We're just doing what molecules do, bumping off each other and saying excuse me and I'm sorry, did I hurt you, and then hitting someone else. All except Ginita Wall. She's all balled up in a dark corner, not making a sound, just scrunched up with her head facing the floor, and her arms around her knees, like she can smell her crotch. Ginita always does something different. If Miss E or Miss M say, "Pretend you're in an elevator and it's stuck between floors and the ceiling is coming down to you, closer and closer, and there's fifteen people in there. What would you do?" Well, anyone would scream. Not Ginita Wall. She'll climb through the trap door and save everybody. Or suppose you're supposed to be improvising you're at a bus station, and everything starts getting real dull or rowdy, which means that Arlin has started picking a fight with someone, Ginita will throw one of her epileptic fits right there in front of the ticket office. Anyone would notice *that*. So, wouldn't you know it, Arlin will be the one to put something in her mouth so she won't swallow her tongue or choke to death, and then he'll put a coat over her, and then he'll brag about it! Well, I guess that excepting for his wings, Arlin *could* become a doctor.

I guess there's all types of molecules. There's Arlin and me, and Ginita. Mama is like Arlin and Miss E is like Ginita and I'm like me. Only I wish I had a sister. Mama told me one day that it was too late for that foolishness. She didn't seem too interested in giving me a sister. She said that Daddy was too old, and she was too tired and no Wembley woman had business begetting after age forty, and here she went and upset the whole scheme, she, having me at age forty-two. "Well, it's just almost too much, Kari Lee," she always says, "Me, Nita Wembley, getting ready to go into middle age with a youngster, something sacrilegious about it. Here me and your Daddy tried for so long, and then I gave up and in my forty-second year, you come along, Kari Lee. Thank God you ain't disfigured! It sometimes happens in your later years. Not that I'm that old, Kari Lee! Oh, was Cloyd surprised! And what about me, nearly done with all that female business and looking forward to your Daddy leaving me alone. Yes, it was a shock! I don't know, I wasn't right *prepared!*"

I don't know what Mama means when she says that; maybe she's just talking. She's got nobody to talk to except herself, and me. Daddy doesn't talk much, all he does is work. Mama too, she works and works, cleaning and renting apartments to people, helping Daddy with his plumbing business and taking care of the house. She says *she's* the reason we live in Oak Hill Estates and are rich.

If space is a solid, then you can cut through it. Your arm is like a knife, and your body is a knife, too, and when you walk, not like normal, all slouched and lazy and kicking things, but as if you're aware and conscious and thinking, you're cutting through space. Your body is a knife. "Try walking like that," Miss E says, "all of you walk in a circle and imagine that you are cutting through space."

Oh, and then Arlin starts playing like he's got an imaginary sword in his imaginary hands and he's cutting space. Ginita just looks at him and she keeps walking around in the circle with a kinda strange but dignified walk like I've never seen her walk, like she's really cutting through space, and I can *almost* see what Miss E is talking about. Whether it's mud or ice or if you're walking on glass or on a hot sidewalk in the summer time with bare feet, or even soft, green grass, keep thinking, "Space is a solid, space is a solid."

"Let's walk in molasses," Arlin says. Me and Ginita Wall just look at each other and then at Arlin. Because of that Pill, with a capital P, everyone has to walk in molasses. Yuck. He *would* say molasses!

"What time is it?" Arlin says, 'cause he's bored.

"Half an hour to go," says Miss M. She keeps watching the time too. Miss M looks bored, maybe she's waiting for that man who meets her after class. He's real dark, probably from another country. "If you're American, marry an American. If you're colored, marry a colored. If you're Chinese, marry a Chinese," Mama says. "None of this other stuff now, no Wembley has ever married anyone but they was from good old West Texas stock. That's the reason we ain't had no disfigurements in this family. Wembleys still Wembleys," Mama says. I wonder who Miss E's boyfriend is. She's *so* pretty!

Oh, that Arlin, he's always so bored! If you're crippled, you get bored easier, that's what Mama says.

"Lay down," Miss E says.

"Me lay down, no way in hell," says Arlin.

Arlin never stays after class to talk to anyone. His Mama picks him up for his karate class, golly, and then he practices on us later!

"You ain't gonna get me to lay down like I was sick," says Arlin, "'cause I'm not sick and I ain't never been sick!"

"You *aren't* gonna get me," I correct.

Arlin stands there and flaps whiles me and Ginita lay down on the rug part of the room and giggle when our toes touch.

"Find a space that's all yours," says Miss E, "spread your arms out."

Gosh, I wonder if hearing things like *that* makes Arlin feel like a worm; well, it's not *his* fault, it's his Mama's, and that drug's.

"Spread out, relax and breathe deeply," says Miss E with a hypnotizing voice. Arlin has *finally* laid down on the boy's side and is play-snoring.

"Find a space that's *yours*, belongs to *you*, and close your eyes."

"Aw, Miss Esquibel, do I have to?" Arlin whispers.

"Close your eyes, Arlin, breathe deeply and imagine you are as small as a molecule. You are becoming smaller and smaller and smaller, until you become so small you can enter your body, which is laying on the floor below you. You are at the top of the ceiling, so small and curious that you can go inside your body easily, a molecule. You go through an orifice . . ."

"Orifice!" shrieks Arlin.

"An eye or an ear or any other place you like," says Miss E.

Arlin snickers when somebody says what an orifice is. For a cripple Arlin sure has a dirty mind.

"Now, wander inside and explore the space. What is it like?"

Arlin snickers again, and then he farts! Everyone laughs and says, "EEEEeeeeeeyyyyywwwwwooooo!" But Miss E says, "Now close your eyes and concentrate. C-O-N-C-E-N-T-R-A-T-E. Now starting from where you are, go through your body, exploring it and seeing and feeling it, and smelling and touching. We're on a body journey this afternoon. No space is too small. No space is too strange or too unfamiliar to us. And if it is unfamiliar, or different, remember how it feels and smells and tastes. Is it dark? Crowded? How do you feel? Now move on."

"Isn't it time to go home?" says Arlin. "I got karate lessons," he mumbles.

Arlin is giggling and my right leg is going to sleep and when I open my eyes, I can see Ginita so relaxed and happy like she *really* is on a body journey and is having a wonderful time. I keep trying, I really do, but I just can't concentrate. I feel too itchy and nervous-like. It's Arlin that's bothering me, not Miss E, 'cause her voice is soft and soothing and she makes me think thoughts I've never felt before. But I just can't concentrate. Golly, I can smell Arlin's feet over here on the girl's side. I *really* am trying to think and remember and then move on, inside my body. I guess that's what Miss E means. Concentrate. Concentrate, Kari Lee. I am. I am. Space is a solid. Space is a solid. Space is a solid.

II
Rocío

It was at this time that my hands started turning blue. I first noticed it going up an elevator to an opening night cast party. Elevators give license to hysterical thoughts. Who hasn't imagined death in an elevator, crushed between floors, bodies piled up in broken heaps, strangers no longer.

Loudon, my boyfriend, stood solidly behind me in his navy blue, wool, army store coat. His beard and long shoulder length hair flowed together in front of his kind, monastic face. Loudon was a radical in search of radicalism. He was going through the Machine, working on his M.F.A. in Drama, that coveted crown of endurance. He was a large ex-football player gone to seed. He'd broken his leg the week before going to Vietnam with the Marines and he continued to limp in memory of his departed brothers, all of them blown up, blown away. Loudon lay a puffy hand on my shoulder, his thick fingers caressed my thin neck thoughtlessly. They were the hands of the self-absorbed dreamer: squared, bitten down.

I stared at the opening between the cushioned elevator doors. "Aren't these pads used in lock-up tanks, Loudon, padded rooms for persons with psychological problems?"

Only the other day I tried on a strait-jacket, my first fitting, in the costume shop. I'd been folding tights all morning in the tiny back room where we kept all the hats and tights and belts and underwear. I'd brought a footstool from the large front room where Solly Mathison was cutting a pattern for himself. "Hey, Solly, I'm going to the back room to fold tights, straighten up back there. Call me if Mrs. Larsen comes up."

"So all right," Solly said, absorbed with his latest creation for himself.

"Hey Ros, see about some feathers back there, red ones. I'm getting this number together, baby. Ros, it is hot shit!" he said, as he held up a satin jumpsuit that plunged to just below his dark nipples. "I got a singing date coming up, check those feathers would you?"

"Solly, you want those earrings I told you about? The left-over, stray ones I've lost?"

"Yeah, baby, slip' em to me, I can dig 'em," he said, "or I knows some people who can use 'em," he muttered, slowly stroking his thin chest and then his left earlobe. "Always looking for a bit of flash, baby!"

"I'm going to the back, call me if . . ."

"Yeah, yeah, yeah, now don't you get naughty back there. 'Well, hello Dolly, hello Dolly, it's so nice to see you back again.' Red feathers, Ros . . . 'I can tell, Dolly . . . You're looking swell, Dolly' . . . far out and if this ain't the hottest piece of shit ever caressed this baby boy's sweet ever loving ass!"

I kicked the footstand back between the racks of costumes that hung in the darkness of the clothing warehouse. Henry VIII's costume clung to a dog's suit while Solange's plaid pinafore and apron soundlessly caressed Charlotte Corday's low-cut summer frock. Two metal racks, one eye-level, the other higher, wound their way to the back of that mausoleum waiting for the day of theatrical resurrection. A bodice here, a shirt there, shoes, and now a coat, and of course, tights, the black ones, with holes that I had so patiently sewn, every other Wednesday from 8:30 to 11:30. It was my duty, my privilege, my honor, to serve the great theatre machine, myself an apprentice in the craft of camouflage.

How far does art go, and when does pure, unadulterated slavery begin? A cup of Amway soap couldn't really clean Jettie Brady's soiled underpants and spotted girdle. As part of my weekly job, I was responsible for washing the actors' clothes and costumes. I climbed down to the second floor the back way, meeting Rolla Larsen, the Costume Mistress, who was carrying a box of turquoise seamrippers in her hands, the kind that Solly Mathison liked to steal. I mumbled something, while Rolla climbed the back stairs. I watched her large pleated ass disappear, and snarled in her direction, still nervously trembling from my morning's breakfast of instant hot chocolate with water. Later I combed through the men's dressing room, extricating once-starched shirts and pairs of brown knickers, and a few dark socks. *The Crucible* was a play about fanaticism, wild passions, but for the time being, its themes were dirty collars, sweat stains and mismatched footwear.

Crossing the stairway, I went into the women's dressing room where I sorted through lingerie, bringing into the light more of Jettie Brady's underclothes. Jettie Brady, the woman with the dyed and thinning blond hair, the long hook nose, the cold dispassionate blue eyes and the yeast-stained panties, was in charge of all apprentices. It was she I was accountable to. How far does art go and when does slavery begin? Jettie Brady was on her witch hunt in the Salem present.

Standing in the elevator with Loudon's huge hands on my neck, I composed a letter in my mind . . .

Dear Jettie:

I have been wanting to talk to you for a long time regarding the feudal conditions in the Costume Shop. Isn't there any way I could be moved to another work-study job here in the theatre? Rolla Larsen is unfair, unkind, dictatorial. I haven't been feeling well, Jettie, I wonder if . . .

I looked down at my hands. I have taken to re-evaluating limbs every five years or so. My once skinny, bony hands with the long fingers now have suddenly become "artistic." The long fingers are elegant, bespeaking acts of creation, works of art. They are the hands of an artist, the creator of worlds.

"My hands are blue. My hands are blue. Loudon, my hands are blue."

"Your hands are blue?" he says.

"God, my hands are blue! Loudon, I have to get out of this elevator."

"Come on, Rocío, just settle down, two floors to go."

"Two floors to go!" Padded hysteria with two floors to go. "My hands have never turned blue before. Oh, they've been cold, Loudon, they're always cold, but this is different! From the wrist down, my hands are blue!"

"Rocío, now just get something to eat, okay?"

The elevator doors opened and Loudon quickly stepped in

front of me and disappeared into the crush of faces at Roland Nevis' party for *The Crucible*. I knew about witch hunts. I faced the supreme Wicca, Lorna Preston, the speech teacher. She looked radiant, her long brown hair flowing on her shoulders, framing a cultured, prepared face. She was the witch, Abigail, regaling men over onion dip and crackers.

"Ma Me Mi Mo Mu," Lorna said in speech class and "The Lawyer's Awfully Awkward Daughter Ought To Be Taught To Draw . . . EEEEEEEEEEEEEEE—YOOOOOOO! Now repeat after me: MMMMEEEEEE; PPPPPPRRRRRRRR-REEEEE; WWWWWWEEEEEEE; ME, ME, ME, PREE, PREE, PREE, WEE, WEE, WEE, and *remember*: Marilyn Monroe lips! Sexy, loose, and relaxed. That's the secret the English speak so well, have you seen their forward stretch? Watch my lips, watch me."

Every day she was the disheveled vituperous bitch; tonight she was Abigail before the fall, long-tressed, bright-faced, with puckered red lips, in a long flowered peasant dress near the cheddar cheese balls.

Ron Lerner waved to me from across the room. He was so handsome, with dark eyes and hair and the innocent, bewildered look of a maligned Lucifer, prior to the moment of banishment. He was beautiful, vainglorious, expectant, hopeful, proud and full of troubled hidden lights. I waved to Ron and he motioned for me to cross to him. He took my hand, not noticing its inky hue. I wanted to forget the illness that crept up my arm, immobilizing goodness and filling me with dread, inquietude and paranoia in the midst of heightened celebration.

"Ron!"

"Come upstairs with me? Come on!"

"Ronald, how are you?"

"Let's go look at the rooms upstairs."

"Can you believe this house?"

"Nice, huh?"

"Have you eaten?"

"The Swedish meatballs."

"Christ, I don't know what I'd do, Ron, if I didn't eat well at these parties. Have you eaten mellorine, that's how bad it's gotten."

"So, let's go upstairs and look at the rooms, Rocío. Still looking for a place to live?'

"Do you know of anything?"

"How about the Robertson complex where Loudon lives?"

"I don't know, I don't want to depend on Loudon, I need my own place. You still at the house on Emmett Hill?'

"Yeah. God, would you look at these rooms. Hey, Rocío, come in here with me."

I stepped inside the master bathroom. I could see myself in the three-way mirror with its veiled patterns of grey rivulets that ran across the mirrors's expanse. The walls were lime green with white trim, the carpets were white and covered with shag fur. The toilet tank cover, the lid cover and the base of the toilet were immaculate with snowy down. The soap dishes exuded lemon-scented freshness. Ron stood behind me. I could see him in the mirror. I am in love with him, I thought. Easily, carelessly, he traced the outline of my shoulder and back with his fingers. I wanted to say, "I love you, Ron. Do you still live in the house on Emmett Hill?" But instead, I cleared my throat, stepped outside.

"I'll be right out," the dark angel said mysteriously.

Ron had locked the bathroom door. I sat in the hallway, waiting for him to exit. I stared at the beige wallpaper with its shadowed coronets. Loudon doesn't understand. I have no home. I am homeless. Where can I move? Why won't Loudon let me stay with him? After all, we are friends. We're *friends*, aren't we? He's too busy, all his time taken up. Why do people get degrees? How many hearts broken, lovers abandoned? Loudon! Where's Ron? I'll just wait here. Sit down. On this loveseat. Alone. Wait for Ron. My hands are blue. Why? I don't know, it's all too much. I don't have a place to live, Loudon doesn't want me, he's told me so.

Dear Jettie:

I just *have* to get out of the Costume Shop, can't

you find me another job? I'm afraid.

Ron! Where are you? What are you *doing* in there? Ron?

Go downstairs to the party and eat something. Swedish meatballs. My hands aren't so blue. Ron. Get out of the bathroom. Get out of there.

From where I sit I can see three doors. One. Two. Three. One of them is dark, one of them leads into another room, the last to the outside

world. But no, we are seven flights up. I'm going downstairs to talk to Loudon. Eat something. My hands aren't so blue. I don't know what to do. Ron, what are you doing in there? The house on Emmett Hill is filled with men. Lucifer is Lord. Ron is a misguided angel. He told me a story of growing up in hotels. Eugene O'Neill and Ron, playwrights born in hotel rooms, trying the rest of their lives to find homes, someone to love. Ron, I love you. Come out of the bathroom and talk to me. You could hold me if you want. That man with the blond beard, Leland, his bumpy chest in a black fishnet shirt, he lives on Emmett Hill; he and Raymond, the other speech teacher, you live with them. Do they make love to you? Ron, do they? Just come out6 of the bathroom and tell me. We'll talk. That's all I need now. Someone to talk to. There are three doors. One. Two. And three.

III
Kari Lee

> This is my line. I've walked it so many dang times I'm getting dizzy. The part that really mixes me up is the part that comes at the beginning, that curved bend on the left that looks like a turkey's red hangy thing—the reason being that I gotta speed up coming out of a spin at that point, and loop around the top part, you could call it the head, and shoosh down, turning right, and then go into a bumpity hop hop hop hopping with a SUDDEN STOP.

My line reminds me of:

> A turkey (I said this before).
> A man's privates (golly, this is my notebook and I'm not sure I want Arlin or even Ms. E to see it—not to mention Mama! She thinks men's privates are dirty and ugly and who would want to see a man naked as a jay-bird except someone sick. She says Michaelangelo was sick and so are most artists. They got a fever can't be cured by anything, not even drugs. Miss E's an artist, but she's not sick. Miss M, well, she's a little funny, but not what you'd call SICK. More like WEIRD. Oh, I don't know, maybe only certain artists are sick, like Michaelangelo and people from the past.

> Miss E said to keep writing down what you think, but I don't know. When you're working with a line, you're not supposed to let your thoughts stop even if they are stupid, 'cause you never know when you might see a flash of light going on in your head, inspiration it's called. "Perspiration is more like it," Arlin says in his snotty way. I keep getting confused and I start thinking about real people and real life and then I start wondering about this and that and about what they think about so and so and what so and so says and like Arlin says, I'm just responding to stimuli.

My line reminds me of:

A turkey—
the top of the turkey head

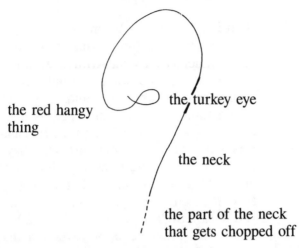

the red hangy
thing

the turkey eye

the neck

the part of the neck
that gets chopped off

Yick. Now why'd I think of a headless turkey? Well, maybe it's okay, 'cause Miss E says to stay with your line, walk it, skip it, hop it, dance it and run it. I did and I got dang tired. Wouldn't you know it, Arlin Threadgill rode his line on a bike! Well, someone had to steady him at first, so it's no fair. The line was probably straight too. It's pretty incredible for a crippled kid like him to ride a line like that!

My line reminds me of:

> Thanksgiving. If you turn it upside down, it looks like an amoeba, kind of, or a fetus that's whiplashing around, or a piece of wet wax that's drying up.

Now I'm getting tired of my line. But what can you do with it, once it's yours? Stick with it—until it has run itself through all it's gonna run through. All you can do is watch and listen and remember. This is my line. This is my line. It came to me. It came out of me. It's me, and now I want it to become even Me-er than Me.

Mama wouldn't understand my line. She has her own lines.

Nobody would understand my line, except maybe Miss E, 'cause she understands things like how a person feels when she walks a line alone—twisting and turning and hopping yourself down to the end—stopping, and then beginning again. Now with sound: MMMMMMMMMMMM-MMMMMMMMMMMMMMMMMMMMMMMM—tut tut tut, ploom.

My line has a sound, a high-pitched cry—revving up and then dying out. Ploom. Ploom. Hard crash. The turkey neck falls to the ground.

My line reminds me of: All I can think are turkey thoughts, dang it!

IV
Rocío

The first time I saw Nita Wembley was the day of the garage sale at her White Oak Street apartments. I'd borrowed Loudon Reiley's car, Cochise, to go apartment hunting. At that time I was living at the Robertson Estates with Loudon, in his bowling alley shaped room, that under it the influence reminded me of an alien space ship. Come in, Captain Reiley, this is attendant Esquibel patching in. TALK TO ME. TALK TO ME. Beam me up to that place so that when we sleep we will travel together in dream.

"Have you ever read Mircea Eliade?"

"No, Loudon, who is she?"

"He! Ritual and Pathos, that sort of thing. Like Artaud."

"God, he was so handsome! What happened?"

"The artist demon in him . . . drugs, sex, bad teeth, the senses, and farther out . . . the greatest masturbatory experience . . . himself as . . ."

"He was so handsome . . ."

"God, Rocío, are you there again? I was there ten minutes ago. Move on, would you? Jump! Your mind needs to jump! You get stuck!"

111

The garage sale consisted of a small rack of women's clothing, a dark crepe de Chine dress, a heavy navy blue pleated
skirt, some children's clothing, pedal pushers, t-shirts, a winter coat with patches on the elbow, tablecloths, potholders in
bright colors and a Persian lamb coat size 8 with the name
Rose Marilyn hand sewn in the lining.

"Why, hello there. Now if that isn't a fit! It's got your name
on it!"

"Rose Marilyn?"

"I'll have you know that this coat here comes directly from
the wife of a Baptist preacher. It's a fact! Now Quinnie Con-
klin, she sent this coat to me. It belonged to her sister-in-law
that died of cancer!"

"Rose Marilyn?"

"The same."

"Well, it's very pretty. Do you have a mirror?"

"Now, you just step in there to the ladies' room, through
the hallway and see if it ain't *you* all over!"

"It *is* pretty!"

"And it fits so well, just like a glove. You need some
gloves?"

"It's really pretty," I yelled from the empty bathroom. The
apartment was bare except for a couch and a few wooden end
tables.

"It's got your name on it, anybody with eyes can see that.
Now looka here, it's a buy, you'd be a fool not to take it at
$10. Now there's a girl! It's just right for you, it's *you* all
over. What you hemming for? Now take it, and that's that!"

Nita Wembley stood near the fireplace at the end of the
large comfortable living room. She was a small woman, with
a wrinkled, pink face. Her lips were incredibly thin, non-
existent almost and devoid of lipstick. She had no makeup on,
and wore a thin grey and black Woolworth scarf on her head
over tiny blue rollers that pulled her wrinkles tightly toward
her scalp. She wore a white men's shirt, buttoned incorrectly,
causing the bottom of the shirt to hang down on one side like
a ragged dog's ear. She was unkempt, in black stretch pants
and once-white, now-grey sneakers with white crew socks.

"My name is Nita Wembley."

"I'm Rocío Esquibel. I'm a graduate student at the Drama Factory."

"You are? Why, maybe you know my little girl, Kari Lee Wembley?"

"Kari Lee Wembley? Is she your daughter? I have her in my Drama Appreciation Class!"

"Why, you're *that* Miss Esquinel! I'd been wanting to meet you. By your name I thought you was Filipino. Why Kari Lee talks about you all the time. Miss Esquinel this and Miss Esquinel that. I declare."

"She's a nice girl."

"Yes, she is. I been sending her to Drama Appreciation class since she was in first. Mr. Wembley and I support the arts. Mr. Wembley is in the 100 Club. Yes, he is. We give regularly to that Factory, we do. We see all the plays, except when Mr. Wembley is working late, or if there is something, you know, not nice in the play."

"You're Kari Lee's mother? It's hard to believe."

"Oh, it is? Yes, I am Kari Lee's mother. I may not look it, but I am her mother. An old woman like me."

"Oh, no, that's not it, I mean, I'm just surprised to meet you!"

"Surprised? Expecting to see someone younger?"

"No, Kari Lee is a nice girl. She's very responsive and she's got a good imagination."

"That's a fact. She gets her imagination from me, not her daddy. Her daddy is another matter. Cloyd, that's Mr. Wembley, he's a doer, he don't have no time for imagination. Why, we've got the largest plumbing and heating business in West Texas. Yes we do! Our heaters are in all those sky-scrapers in downtown Fort Worth, and we done the plumbing! Mr. Wembley and me, we built up our business outa hard work, Miss Esquinel."

"Esquibel."

"Miss Esquinel."

"Rocío."

"Miss Esquinel, we worked hard, slaving year in and year

113

out. It ain't a fancified business that places you in the front of society people with the Nevis-Springham name and ritzy parties. Me and Mr. Wembley are doers, we done it all, and now there's Kari Lee to carry on. She come along when we didn't expect her and that is a fact! Maybe you're surprised, but Kari Lee is my natural born daughter, she's not adopted. Now what business a woman my age doing having children? I'll tell you, Miss Esquinel. *None.* But the Lord manifested Himself. And that's that. It ain't easy, Miss Esquinel, me, a middle-aged woman, having worked hard all my life. Mr. Wembley works at the office and I run these here apartments. I am constantly cleaning up for the slobs that move in and out like vermin. One day I came in and found a mattress on this very floor and I said to myself, 'Nita Wembley, you get those hippies out of here this minute. I don't care what it takes. You get those dirty hippies out of here before they start having wild sex-filled parties and start smoking mary-wana and doing God knows what. Soon they'll be sleeping on the floor in one heap on that there mattress.' No, I'm too old to change, and too tired and too worn out and too much of a Christian woman to let no hippie atheists vandalize my apartments that I done worked so hard for all my life. Here I am, Lordy me, an older woman with a small child to take care of. You can imagine my surprise when Kari Lee came along. I'm fifty-one years old, Miss Esquinel."

"Why, you're young!"

"No, Miss Esquinel, I'm old. An old woman, working out her last years. The Lord saw fit to send me a child and not only that, but a cross to bear in my later years."

"The apartment is vacant?"

"After all these years of hard work, me and Cloyd moved out to Oak Hill Estates. You know where that is? It's where the rich people live. And Miss Esquinel, we're rich! Little Kari Lee will inherit it all, because I tell you, I'm too tired and too worn out and too old and Cloyd ain't much better off. And what with my cross, it's a heavy life, it is."

"Are you looking for a tenant?"

"Kari Lee came first and then my cross, oh, the Lord

knows why, I don't. Miss Esquinel, now, how do I look to you?"

"Fine, just fine, Mrs. Wembley."

"I don't look sick now?"

"Oh, no, you look just fine."

"Now, you forget the curlers and the clothes and look at me. Look at me. Real close. See anything wrong?"

"No, I . . . no . . ."

"Miss Esquinel, I don't have no breasts."

"You . . ."

"I am without the breasts the good Lord gave me. First Kari Lee and then, well, can you see, Miss Esquinel, after a life of working hard, God should send me this tribulation from the land of Cain."

"I'm . . ."

"Oh no, no, no, no . . . don't you be sorry. Sorry ain't enough. After all these years, sorry ain't enough. Now, to look at me. anyone would see a normal woman. Do you know what it's like to have your female flesh cut away from you? Now I worked hard, I moved us from nowhere to the Oak Hill Estates. We got a nice fancy house full of pretty things and Cloyd handles all the skyscrapers' accounts and we give to the Drama Factory. We are patrons. We belong to the 100 Club. Miss Esquinel, I believe in dreaming yourself something that you ain't. Now, Kari Lee, she's a good bright girl, she's gonna inherit all of this. Well, sorry ain't enough. It just ain't enough. And that's that."

V
Kari Lee

Miss E and M spread out a huge piece of butcher paper and then brought out a box full of cloth and sequins and felt and stuff like that. Me and Ginita Wall shared scissors and sat next to each other, our knees touching, almost, and kinda smiling and laughing to ourselves.

"These are going to be our texture sheets," says Miss M.

"Texture sheets, are you kidding me?" shrieked Arlin.

"What for?"

"On these sheets we design images from our minds. We'll take the cloth and rope and sequins and make a texture sheet for our characters."

"I don't like my character."

"It's all right, Arlin, we'll work on it today. That's the karate black belt, right?"

"I don't want to do anything dumb in class."

"Let's give it a try. Now everyone, you can do whatever you want with your sheets. Put down the textures that you think your character might like or dislike. You can write down your thoughts on your sheet and color with the crayolas too, just get your images down on paper."

"I ain't got no images," Arlin said.

"I don't have any images," I corrected.

"Golly, Ginita, but I wonder what I'll do about my character. I don't know if I should do likes or dislikes. Dang, if it ain't a turkey. I never could think of anything else for my nature study, so I guess I'll just have to have turkey images. So here goes. Turkeys like warm, tidy, turkey textures and soft earth and bird seed and . . . I hate turkeys!"

"Just put down what you feel, Kari Lee," said Miss E.

"I don't feel nothing, Miss E, except bored," said Arlin.

"Me neither, Miss E," I said. "Oh, I don't feel bored, I mean, I just don't feel nothing one way or another about this dang turkey."

Ginita was jumping around all over the room and getting this and that for her texture sheet and it looked so nice already, it was full of lace and flowers. She's lucky, she's got a human character. Animals are hard. And dumb!

"Just go over to the texture box and feel things, Kari Lee, you might get some texture ideas."

So I went over and stuck my hand in and I felt something wet and sticky.

"AAAAAhhhhh!"

"What is it?"

"Miss E, Arlin put his old spitty waddy bubble gum in the texture box. And I touched it! Yucko!"

"Har har har," laughed Arlin, that PILL. He musta petooied it in with his lips. Anyway, what business did he have in the texture box, he don't got no hands, I wanted to say, but I didn't. Instead I just went back to my spot on the floor and drew a turkey like I always draw turkeys, by outlining my hands with its bumpy, ridgey fingers and then I filled in the spaces between the fingers with a wavy, webby line. Then I worked on the turkey head, drawing a nose or beak, and added a sequin eye, and then I cut up some material in different colors, brown and red and blue and filled in the turkey body. It wasn't too hard after all. Ginita was working on her laces and pearls and I was with my turkey feathers and Arlin was over in the corner not even texturing anything. All he was doing was practicing karate kicks like he was Bruce Lee with arms. He got tired after awhile and sat down and looked kinda sad and, for the first time, I almost felt sorry for him. I must admit that by the end of the class, I was pooped too, but "Tom" was done, and I gave him to Miss E and she liked it well enough.

After class, Miss E and I sat together near the coke machines talking while I was waiting for Mama to come and get me. Miss E said, call me Rocío, and do you know I'm living at your mother's apartment on White Elm Street? It's real nice. I just got a cat, too, but don't tell your Mama, 'cause I'm not supposed to have cats. I said, I won't, and she says, I'll tell her about the cat soon. Her name is Oriene and she's a Calico. Someday you'll see her. Your texture sheet is really something, Kari Lee, you're the only one in Drama Appreciation III class that's picked an animal to texture and character. That's something! Animals—they know, they feel, they respond and they love. I said yes, I know. They're smart, she said, because they're quiet and listen, and maybe even remember. They're like molecules, I said, they have space and lines and a texture. And they love you, quietlike and without reproach, said Miss E with a dreamy stare. For always, I said. Yes, said Miss E. Gosh, I thought to myself, but Miss E's texture is so nice.

Bye now, Kari Lee, you take care and say hello to your Mama. See you next week. That's what Miss E said to me after class when we were sitting next to the coke machine near the stairs going up to the theatre lobby. No one was around but us two, eating melty Butterfingers that Miss E had in her purse. We washed the pieces down with cold Dr. Peppers, and talked about nothing, anything and everything.

VI
Rocío

November the 10th. Walked back from the theatre in darkness. The end of another day of slavery, albeit self-imposed. I stopped in the park near White Elm Street, and watched the sky for traces. There were a few stars and they occasionally peeped through that great vast sky like oiled beads. I'm tired. Class 8:30 to 11:30, lunch and then work on Ionesco's *War Games*. In one scene a dying person reaches out; no one is there, but he imagines invisible arms holding him. He is consoled and peacefully evicts his tortured flesh. Next to him a woman cries out in terror, hold me, hold me, I'm afraid and it's dark! Hold me. She is smothered with touches, caresses, her lover, her family nearby. She imagines she is alone, dies, crying out.

I found a dead bird next to the park bench. The darkened grass was wet, my feet sank into the earth. I spun around, hearing someone. I didn't have a car. Someone called out—a stranger, "Hey, hey you!" I was afraid, walked briskly toward home. I wrapped the dead blackbird in white notebook paper.

Bury it, Rocío. Bury it.

The overhead stars were obscured by clouds. They were bright sinkholes, pulling light. I imagined that a passing plane was a space ship, with its flashing lights. I wanted to be taken. Freed.

Instead, I quickly walked the remaining blocks to the Wembley house. Joe's light was on; he was studying or eating supper by himself. I am in love with Joe, his blond strength, his violet eyes, his sureness and his sorrow. Joe was married, to someone in the theatre, but he found her in bed with someone else. May you never live to see the day. He doesn't talk about it, Loudon said to me. Joe was his best friend, Joseph Pappas, the actor with the thinning hair, the long legs, Joseph eating alone, his bright light in the window. My next door neighbor, Joe, to me the other day, "Wembley's crazy, Rocío, remember that!"

"Joe," I said, "but I need a place to live! At least you're a man and she doesn't bother you. Does she go on about her breasts to you? I can't take it anymore!"

"She's gone on enough to me, but her breasts, God forbid, no!"

"Only a woman," I said, "would inflict herself on another woman that way."

"She's crazy, all right," he said, whistling in disbelief.

"It's Kari Lee I feel sorry for."

"Oh yeah, her."

Joe moved toward the door of his small apartment. I wanted to peer inside, be invited over, but it was unthinkable. I was Loudon's girl, and after what Joe had been through, with his ex-wife, the scenes, the infidelity, the confrontation, all of which I had vividly imagined, a cup of tea was impossible.

"See you, Joe."

"Just remember what I told you, Rocío, the woman's mad! Just remember that and pay your rent on time."

The dead bird lay on the back porch. I fumbled for the key. I scavenged through my purse, impatient and talking to myself. No key. I'd have to break in. But how? The last time I'd used a dinner knife I'd found on the ground near the house. The knife was cold and it had slipped from my grasp and cut me in the upper lip. I bled profusely, cursing Loudon Reiley, "Damn him, damn him" all the way back to the Robertson Estates. Crying "Loudon Loudon Loudon why won't you help me." The knife was nearby and the window was fixed. Damn Loudon for fixing the damn window. I broke through the glass window again, shards flew about me, falling to the wooden porch with a tinkle.

Bury it, Rocío. Bury it all. The dead bird was waiting. Now, *that* was the problem. One of the problems. Nita Wembley let me move into her apartment even though she knew I was poor. I received two hundred dollars a month stipend and the rent was two hundred dollars a month.

"Miss Esquinel, the first month you can pay one hundred. I'll help you out, how about that?"

"Why, Mrs. Wembley, that's so nice of you! Yes, it would really help me out, after that I'm sure . . ."

"Well, after that is a time from now."

"Yes."

"I'm doing this 'cause of Kari Lee and her drama education, mind you."

It was now the 10th of November and my second month's rent was past due, but I had no money until the end of the month. I should call Mrs. Wembley, but what would I say? Could Loudon, no, not Loudon, never Loudon. As far as my family was concerned, they'd already sent me a hundred and I was too ashamed to ask for more.

"And 'cause I'm a Christian woman, Miss Esquinel."

As I opened the door, my schizophrenic pregnant cat escaped. Damn the cat! She'll come back to eat. They all come back hungry after screeching fuck me fuck me in the glowing darkness.

I turned on the light; it was late, about ten p.m. Loudon was at home, working on his thesis. Stoned with grass and music and himself. I dug a hole in the cold ground close to the house and buried the dead bird, covering it with moist earth. Then I took the once silver-plated rusty knife inside. This was the last time. A memento of struggle that I wanted to keep. In the refrigerator there was cat food and cold leftover macaroni.

I could hear Joe next door, practicing speech exercises. MA ME MI MO MU. He was Y-buzzing his way to fulfillment.

Having buried the dead bird, having washed my blue

hands, having attempted to eat supper, I lay down.

Dear Jettie:

I'm not feeling well. That is the reason for not attending class all last week. It's hard to explain. I can't eat. I choke on my food. My hands keep turning blue. Recently, I've started falling down stairs. I have no strength in my legs, I keep falling down. I thought I broke my ankle the other day on the goat path behind the theatre, but now I'm feeling better. I'm tired. God, I'm just so tired.

Oriene was meowing outside. When I let her in she followed me to bed, both of us shivering. She was very pregnant and huddled by my side. I looked down to where she lay moaning on my stomach. She was oozing a brown bile; her juice was all over my blanketed stomach. She was frightened and looked at me, whimpering. She didn't know what was happening. Was it possible? Cats know instinctively, don't they? Oriene was scared, birthing already in my lap. I picked her up, looked at her closely and said softly, "You must." I placed her in the large closet in the hallway. Inside I had already arranged a bed for her. It was a straw mat covered by a sheet. She went to it, uncomprehending still. Oriene! Oriene! If only I could . . . which reminded me of Ionesco's play. I thought of the dying man and woman. I ran my fingers over my forehead and face. Tired skin. Tired. Tired.

YYYYYYYYYYYYYYYYYYYYYYYYYYYYYYYYYY-YYYYYY———OOOOOOOOOOOOOOOOOOOOOOOOO!

Joe's voice shrieked through the walls. YYYYOOOO!! And now I heard the Irish brogue that signified clarity. Now if we could forget. Was it possible? Loudon was working on his thesis. It was a play about communicating without words. Forgive the many transgressions, as I forgive you, reach out and feel hands, warm and full of blessed understanding. Hands that allow this leave-taking without demanding more than the dying can give. Even at the moment of traveling through space to the Captain's side. Signaling. Signaling.

What? That you were there before Loudon, that he was left behind, this time. I turned off the overhead light, my head buzzing in the silence. I got up and wrote in my journal:

> The blindness of white on white
> the moss of tree on tree
> plant over plant, flowing
> the liquid green—
> my silence—
> was crying
> to throw itself
> down

and then

> Sorrowed death trance of fear
> living
>
> Remember the funny lady
> with the little blue hat
>
> Texas in April
> was one time
>
> Climbing up flights
> going down to Holy Places
> around the block
>
> Impaled, we
> were.

VII
The Wembleys

"Open the door. It's Miss Esquinel a ringing. I saw her from the window. She's a Spanish girl. You know what pretty hair their people have."

"Esquibel, Mama! She's so pretty and so nice and all the kids like her, they do, Mama!"

"Kari Lee Wembley, you open that door! Miss Esquinel's waiting. She may be nice, but she's two weeks late with her rent."

"Mama, I'll get it!"

"Well, go on then, get the door!"

"Miss E!"

"Kari Lee!"

"Hi."

"Ask Miss Esquinel in, Kari Lee."

"I really can't stay long, Mrs. Wembley. I just came by to bring the rent. I'm sorry I'm late but . . ."

"It's all right now, you just step in here and sit down, Miss Esquinel."

"Oh, Mrs. Wembley, your house is lovely! It's really lovely!"

"It's a pretty house, there's no denying. Now get out of the way Kari Lee and let Miss Esquinel look around."

"It's really nice, Mrs. Wembley."

"Yes it is. I worked hard for all of this, I'll have you know, all my life I worked to move into this neighborhood, and no one's gonna take me from it, exceptin' the Good Lord when he calls me home."

"You want to sit down, Miss E?"

"The name's Esquinel, Kari Lee, you call her *Miss* Esquinel."

"I told all the kids to call me Rocío, or Miss E, Mrs. Wembley."

"Now, do you think that's right, Miss Esquinel, all that familiarity? Now come over here to this couch, won't you?"

"I wanted to come by and tell you how sorry I am for not bringing the rent sooner. I got busy at school. Mrs. Wembley, I *really* am grateful to you for letting me live in the apartment. It's lovely, so nice and clean."

"How's Oriene, Miss E?"

"Oriene, who's that, Kari Lee? I *did* rent that apartment to a bachelor girl, Miss Esquinel!"

"It's her cat, Mama!"

"All my places are clean, Miss Esquinel. I clean 'em

123

myself. Look at my hands. They're ugly. They are. I've worked them hard. I don't hire no one to clean my places. I clean them myself, no fancy maids for me, and I clean my own house, and it's big. I done it all by myself in the past. I'll do it by myself in the future. So, you watch that animal, young woman."

"It's a beautiful house."

"Yes it is. Kari Lee, you got any homework?"

"Mama, hardly none."

"Now, run along and play. I want to talk to Miss Esquinel alone."

"Mama, I got hardly nothing to do and it's almost supper-time."

"Now Kari Lee Wembley, don't you be crossing me, go and do your homework."

"Aaaaaaaaaaaright, Mama. Bye, Miss E, see you next week, okay? I've been working on my nature study gobs. My turkey, remember?"

"That's wonderful, Kari Lee! See you later."

"Bye."

"She's such a nice girl."

"Yes, she is. But I don't know, Miss Esquinel, I have to tell you, it's a difficulty having a youngster when a person's already tired out. She ain't no trouble to me and Cloyd, that's Mr. Wembley, but all the same, it's not easy and then there's my cross. I never suspected the Lord smite me for my sins. It's the truth, I done all I could all my life, working hard building up the plumbing business with Cloyd and to have the Lord . . ."

"I brought the rent."

"Just leave it there on that coffee table, Miss Esquinel. We got everything we need or want, Miss Esquinel. Kari Lee ain't lacking for a thing!"

"Ooooh," Nita Wembley sighed, then placed both hands on her vacant breasts. "It's a cross same as I breathe." Nita started to cry, the dried, long withheld tears of someone who hadn't cried in years. "I never cry much, must be the tired-ness."

"Mrs. Wembley, you'll be okay. You're alive and you have a family that loves you."

"You a churchgoer?"

"I am . . ."

"Catholic, like all your people?"

"You're so lucky, Mrs. Wembley, you have so many things to be thankful for, your work, this house, Kari Lee . . ."

"Ohhhh Lord!" Nita Wembley called out. She fingered the buttons on her blouse. She was dressed in a man's blue work shirt with a pair of soft-looking, much-washed jeans and the same grimy pair of tennis shoes. Her hair was in tight curls, like a little girl's. She wore no makeup. Her dried transparent skin resembled the stretched leather of thirsty, dying animals. Her face showed the meanderings of riotous veins. She looked bad, a dessicated, old dog with an empty look of unnamed longing. She unbuttoned her work shirt, pulled up her faded white t-shirt and showed me her ravaged breasts.

I sat in the brilliant fading sunlight of early evening, facing Nita Wembley's pinched, scarred, inverted chest. She looked at me closely, then looked at her breasts with contempt.

"You're a child," she said. "The Lord spare you this."

Slowly, she lowered her t-shirt, buttoned her work shirt, tucked it in with a calloused finger and sat facing me. A cloud rambled past the room and it grew dark. The tables and lamps cast long shadows on the walls. The ashtrays, ornaments and cut glass figurines exuded a crystalline composure. The room was silent, large. I fingered the rent envelope, cleared my throat.

Nita Wembley faced me.

"Me, working hard all my life . . . for this . . ." she said with disgust and horror.

Cochise was waiting outside. Loudon was writing his play on the other side of town.

Just then a man entered the room. Mrs. Wembley turned on a huge, three-way table lamp that was positioned near her; our island was furnished now with light.

"Cloyd Wembley, Kari Lee's daddy."

Mr. Wembley nodded to me courteously, saying nothing.

"It's very nice to meet you, Mr. Wembley."

"Now Cloyd, you go on back and clean up and I'll get you supper."

I stared into Cloyd Wembley's face, having stood to shake his hand. He was a lean, weathered man with a bulbous nose covered with enormous blackheads of some fifty years standing. They were dark and large, blocking innumerable pores. They were plugs the likes of which are rarely seen. Cloyd Wembley wore dark-grey work clothes, a green-striped work cap and work boots. His large, hairy arms were splattered with tiny flecks of mud and dried cement. When he took off his hat, I could see the marks of rimmed sunburn and sweat attesting manual labor outdoors. His hair was plastered-down, sweaty-looking and full of dandruff. He smelled like an overheated goat: acrid, meaty.

The handshake was quick, firm and left me with moist fingers.

"Now Cloyd, you go on. Clean up."

Cloyd Wembley bowed and walked to the back of the house. He had a quiet dignity that had not been killed by his wife of thirty-six years, try as she had, the shrill, long-suffering Nita Wembley, née Humphries.

"That's Mr. Wembley. Man's a mess now."

"Mrs. Wembley, I'd better go."

"I know."

"Thank you."

"I'll show you to the door, Miss Esquinel. Time for Mr. Wembley's supper."

"Your house is lovely. Really. Oh, and by the way, I'll be leaving for Christmas vacation in a few weeks. Joe is going to look after things."

"Yes, it is a nice house," she said, looking around appreciatively.

"I'll be more prompt on the rent payment next month."

"Now you watch that cat, Miss Esquinel. Cats got a foul body smell you let them run wild and scratch the chairs and furniture, not to mention them doing the necessities on the floor and rugs."

"She's a well-behaved cat, trained."

"No wild animal is ever completely trained. People tell me they gonna keep their pet on a leash and I find doggie-do in the corners when I clean up. Had to fumigate the rugs and call in someone to help me, it was so bad one time. You gonna take the cat home with you?"

"No, I've asked Joe to feed her."

"Joe Pappas gonna feed her?"

"Goodbye, Mrs. Wembley, if I don't see you, Merry Christmas!"

"You watch that animal! No tenant of mine is gonna run wild with their animals, it's the same as living in filth!"

"Thank you again!"

I raced down the steps, my knees secure, no problem now of falling down, back to the comforting metallic barriers of Cochise. Nita Wembley waved to me and went inside her Oak Hill mansion. I sat in Cochise, breathing hard, all the windows raised. I was trembling, sick, anxious with the overwhelming weight of Nita Wembley's vile, unstable confessions of guilt and pain. Twenty-five shopping days till Christmas.

VIII
Rocío

"Want some?"

"No, Loudon, I'm too nervous to smoke."

"Forget it, R, let it go."

"I can't. I feel so empty, so helpless."

"Listen to some music."

"Have you eaten, Loudon?"

"No, you want some food?"

"I'm hungry, but I'm too tired to swallow."

"What *is* your problem?"

"I'm just tired."

"You're always tired."

"Yes, I am."

"Damn it, stop crying."

"Loudon, I . . ."

"You can stay here tonight. You want to stay here tonight, Rocío?"

"I don't know, I'm just so tired."

"Why don't you do something about it, see a doctor?"

"I don't have any money. If I could just stop, rest, get away from things. I'm so tired and empty and alone. I'm so depressed."

"Go to bed then."

"Just hold me, would you?"

"Rocío, you okay?"

"Yeah, I'm okay, I'll go to bed. Sleep."

"You aren't hungry?"

"Got something soft? Something I can eat and not think about swallowing?"

"Milk?"

"Yeah, I'll get it. You want some?"

"Sit here, Rocío, you gotta get yourself together. Jettie was telling me that you've been missing class, that you're never in school. *What* have you been doing?"

"Sleeping. I'm just so tired, I can't get up."

"Are you sick?"

"I don't feel good. Most of all, I'm just tired and empty. Like if nothing was inside."

"Rocío, honey, go to bed. Okay?"

"I haven't fed Oriene and the kittens."

"She can wait until tomorrow."

"Loudon, I'm sorry I'm not feeling . . ."

"Yeah, it's okay, just go to bed! I have some work to do, my advisor is waiting for a new draft on the introductory chapter."

"I can go home."

"No, you can stay tonight."

"I'm sorry that you had to move your papers."

"It's okay."

"Really, I can go. Would you give me a ride, I'm so tired."

"Rocío!"

"All right, I'll stay. Goodnight, Loudon, I love you."

"Go to bed!"

Sometimes when I lie down in the spaceship I am frightened. I feel voices on either side, converging in the middle of my head, splitting me apart. Loudon is the first man I have ever lived with; if only he would let me live with him. He is the first man I have slept with, if only he would sleep with me now, my body fully against him, the two halves of a whole. If only he weren't so heavy. When he lays his arm on me, I say, "Loudon, Loudon, your arm, move it. It's too heavy." He complains bitterly and mutters, "What's *wrong* with you?"

"I'm tired, that's all."

If I could just rest. When I fall asleep I hear voices and they talk to me and I see faces, faces of people I know, except they aren't the real faces, but the faces of impostors, all of them, and yet I want to believe. I want to believe!

"You're always so tired," he says.

"I'm so tired of being tired!"

I want to believe. I want to believe. I want to believe!

When I woke up the next morning, Loudon was peering out the window, secretively, furtively.

"Goddamn fucking bitch! Hasn't got any fucking decency. Parading out there for everyone to see!"

"What is it, Loudon? What's going on?"

"Out there in her god damn underwear for all the world to see!"

"What?"

"Standing out there throwing her garbage."

"Who is it?"

I stared out the window across to the vacant parking lot next door to the Robertson Estates. A woman was out there in her white bra and panties throwing garbage. I couldn't make out who she was. I was still unsteady on my feet and bleary-eyed.

"It's Charene," Loudon said contemptuously, at the same time craning his neck to see her as best he could.

"That's Charene? In her underwear? Throwing out the garbage?"

"She does it all the time."

"Loudon, I'm going to school. I wondered if you could

stop in and check in on Oriene and the kittens. You know, feed them."

"I can't do that, R, my thesis."

"Oh," I said limply, going to my clothes.

"You okay today?"

"I'm hungry, you hungry?"

"Eat some eggs."

"Loudon, what do you think is *wrong* with me?"

Loudon was at the window, staring out, the curtain folded suspiciously in front of his face, allowing him to see and not be seen.

"Christ," he said emotionally, "Goddamn fucking whore. Here she comes again. More garbage!"

IX
Nita

That filthy animal smell of cat! I couldn't hardly make it in the door and then I see cat food all over the kitchen floor and then I see the curtains all torn up and hanging there, and on checking the other rooms, I see four cats in there with the big one, the mama, them all stretched out comfortable as can be. She lied to me, the filth and the smell and the cats like all those hippie people trashing out a decent Christian place and not paying the rent on time this month or the last and me finally having to go down there and demand my honest hard-earned money and here I says, me, trusting you and you lying to me and messing this place up and me trying to help you, and giving you a chance, I knowed you didn't have the full rent that first month, so I tried to help you, give you a break, on account of you being Kari Lee's Drama Appreciation III teacher and me thinking you was different than the rest like the time you came over and talked and I shared with you certain things. But you're not so different after all. Well I can tell you this, young woman, I'll call Mr. Trevor at the school and tell him, bet you I will. I'll tell him, being the head of the Drama Factory, about the rent and the apartment and the cats and how you lied to me and that you ain't fit to be in school studying dramatics much less teaching children. You'll be sorry you ever came to know Nita Wembley.

I worked hard all my blessed life, I can't say this enough, and it ain't just all the troubles and the sorrows and the coming of Kari Lee and then my cross and then those hippies with the little baby and now you—a supposed LADY, but underneath, all the same, hippies full of filth. It's something else. And about that you know nothing. Nothing!

I'll call Mr. Trevor and tell him all about you and how you lied to me, and me, unsuspecting, showing you the cup of human kindness, more than human kindness. You'll be sorry you ever ran into Nita Humphries Wembley. Me, a Christian God-fearing woman, someone who tries to help her fellow man and woman, someone who's worked hard all her life and knows what it is to struggle every single day.

Well I tell you now, sorry ain't enough!

X
Rocío

Charene called to me as I walked up the stairs to the Costume Shop. It was Wednesday.

"Rocío!"

"Hello, Charene."

"What's this I hear about you not paying your rent and trashing out Mrs. Wembley's apartment during Christmas break?"

"What?"

"I heard you let your cats run loose in the house and they managed to tear up all the furniture and shred the curtains."

"What? Who told you that?"

"Now look here, Rocío, I'm telling you now that you better get your act together or you're going to be out on your ass. You'll have to start really thinking about what you're doing. Do you know that Mrs. Wembley's one of the theatre's patrons, she's a Golden Angel and Mr. Wembley is in the 100 Club and *that* means that she can do and say anything she damn well pleases around here and that we here at the theatre listen to her? Do you understand that, Rocío? That means that you better the fuck get your priorities and problems and shit together and stop screwing around with members of the 100 Club. Do you understand me?"

"Now Charene, just a minute! I don't see that this is any of your business."

"It *is* my business as house manager of this theatre and don't you forget who you're talking to."

"I don't think you know very much about this."

"I know about you, and how you've been skipping class and carrying on. Jettie and Mr. Trevor told me. I talked to Jettie and she says, if you don't start going to class soon, they're going to kick you out on your ass, so you better watch it, you aren't the person to be messing around with me or Mr. Trevor or Nita Wembley."

"Who told you about this?"

"Get your shit together and stop acting like you're so helpless. Do you hear me?"

"Now just a minute, Charene, let me explain!"

"Goddammit, do you hear me, stop fucking around!"

"How did you hear all of this?"

"Mrs. Wembley called Mr. Trevor."

"She did?"

"Do you understand me? Do you? NITA WEMBLEY IS A GODDAMN FUCKING GOLDEN ANGEL AND IN THE FUCKING 100 CLUB AND NO ONE, NOT EVEN YOU, BITCH, FUCKS WITH HER. Got it?"

Charene Easterman gave me a disgusted look and stomped up the stairs into the lobby where she was to lead a tour of French diplomats around the theatre. She was a native speaker. Ooohhhh mais oui! Charene looked radiant. She was a physically beautiful woman, well-endowed, with golden blond hair. With her back to me, she smiled to the crowd.

I climbed upstairs to the Costume Shop, sidestepping Rolla Larsen who was arguing with Solly Mathison, accusing him of stealing fabric from the costume shop for his own personal use. I entered the darkness of the Clothing Room, found my way past the clothing racks, humid with lost words, indecisive acts, and sat in the small room in the back, on a metal stool, folding tights, sat in silence, too tired to cry.

XI
Loudon

Rocío said, "Take me to Albertson's so I can get things for tonight." Joe was coming over for tacos, Rocío's specialty, and she wanted it to be a good meal. When we got to Albertson's she was afraid to go inside, she said the lights were too bright and she didn't know if she could make it in. And once she got inside, she said, "Loudon, I have to get out. I can't breathe, I need some fresh air."

So, she went outside and stood by the automatic door, looking pale and nervous.

"What's wrong with you," I said, "go and see a doctor!"

And then she started to cry.

"Oh, just give me a list of the things you need and I'll get them."

"No, I've got to do it," she said. "Don't leave me, Loudon, I'm sick."

She went to lie down after we got home and she was crying and then she got up and said, "Hold me."

"Maybe you should lie down," I said, and she was still crying.

"No, no, no, if I lie down I'll die. I don't want to die. I have to make tacos."

She kept saying something about the play she was working on, and about dying alone, even if someone was there, and that scared me. I knew she wasn't all right then, but hell, she wouldn't eat anything and she was skinny as can be, and nervous. Very nervous. There she was, standing over the stove mashing the taco meat and chopping onions and running around and every once in a while she would lie down, but then she'd spring up and start mashing again. She seemed to be okay after a while. Joe came over with his new girlfriend, and the food was good and I stayed there overnight to see if R was okay. The next day she decided to move out of her Oak

Street apartment, and said, "I really shouldn't have a cat, poor thing, it's not fair, she's as crazy as me."

So that next weekend we drove Cochise into the country to her cousin's and R found homes for all the kittens, and then she moved to an apartment on Bowser Street for seventy-five a month. Oh, it's lousy and dark. She says the bathroom is full of spiders. I don't like to go over there unless I have to, but I didn't tell her that. She says she mostly just sleeps there and it doesn't matter. She walks to school from there. Most of the time she stays with me nights and goes home to change. Her mother called over to my place the other night and I heard R explain to her all that had happened. She told me later that her mother had told her (being on a hot line for sick people) that she, Rocío, had had a nervous breakdown, almost. "Aw come on," I said, "are you kidding me? No way, man!"

"It's the little things that go wrong and they just keep adding up," she said, "until one day something really little happens. It might not really be that little, but then it doesn't matter anymore. And then you just disappear. You disappear."

"Hell, Rocío, you're okay, what are you talking about?"

And she turned to me and said, "If it weren't for the tacos, Loudon, I don't know *how* I could have made it."

XII
Kari Lee

Today in class Miss E says we're going to write. Maybe it will help our Nature Study.

"What we're going to write is something about the History of A Friendship."

Miss E talks about a friend—a real close friend—Ramona somebody who got mad at her, I guess that's what happened, Miss E says, 'cause she never really knew for sure, but one day Ramona wouldn't talk to her and ever since then, she's still barely even said hello. "I've tried to be nice and still, she doesn't talk to me," Miss E said. "I called her up several times, but someone else answered and when I left a message for her to call me back, she was at a tennis class, she never answered."

This made Miss E sad and her voice was kinda quavery and for once Arlin Threadgill was quiet and listening.

"And so what happened?" asked Arlin.

"Nothing, except that I guess I'll try again someday. Have any of you ever felt that way?" she said.

Miss E looked so pale and sick, she was out of class for a couple of weeks and she just came back today. Arlin said she was *real* sick.

"So, how'd you find out, creep?"

"My mother told me, double triple creep."

So we talked about it in the hallway and for the second time *ever* I looked at Arlin Threadgill and he wasn't a crippled boy, he was normal-like. And I felt sad. I could still hear my Mama saying mean things about Miss E, things like, "Kari Lee, you stay away from that hippie. You stay away. She's done your Mama harm. I tried to be her friend, Kari Lee, but she lied to me. She's filth, she's filth."

"Oh Mama!" I cried in my room later, "but she's my *friend*. She's my *friend!*"

"Ain't you mine, Kari Lee Wembley?"

"Yes," I said, "oh yes, but Mama, you don't understand, she and I are molecules."

And then Miss E's voice said, "Has it ever happened to you that you think you have a friend and you don't?"

"Yes," I said, and so did Ginita Wall.

"Well, let's write about that. Tell me about a friendship of yours, maybe it was happy and maybe it was sad. Maybe it's like me and Ramona, something went wrong, except one person just can't figure it out."

"Oh, all right," says Arlin.

"Does anyone need any help?" says Miss E.

"Not me," says Arlin, "have I got a story . . ."

"I'm sure it is, Arlin! That's good, that's very good!"

Ginita Wall raised her hand and asked politely, "Miss E, can we use space and line and texture and anything we want with our stories?"

"Of course, Ginita," Miss E said, sitting down. "Now while you're writing *your* stories, I'll write *mine*. Everyone got a pencil?"

"I got a pen," said Arlin.

Everybody found their own very special alone place. Miss E looked at me like she liked me so much, but I turned away 'cause I remembered what Mama told me about Miss Esquibel and I felt sad and sick.

I don't know. I can never think when it comes down to the thinking part. I guess I'll just have to jump in and see what happens. I felt hot and kinda sick and something else that I couldn't describe. I decided to start my thinking again. Miss Esquibel was all hunched up, chewing on a pencil, and thinking real hard. I don't know. I don't know. She looked so busy writing. Once she looked up in my direction, kinda wild-eyed, not really seeing me, but looking out past me, as if she was concentrating on something real hard. You know that wild-eyed look of someone concentrating. So I looked down at my paper and with a kinda shaky hand wrote:

HISTORY OF A FRIENDSHIP
By Kari Lee Wembley
Theatre Appreciation III Class
KARI LEE WEMBLEY   =   6
ROCIO ESQUIBEL   =   6

And I thought to myself, "If Space is a Solid, then what is the Shape of Darkness?"

Compadre

Compadre

I

"Llévale un vaso de agua."

"What?"

"Take him a glass of water."

"What?"

"Take Regino a glass of water, Rocío."

"Where is he?"

"Outside in the backyard. It's hot!"

"We don't have ice. The freezer is jam-packed; a tray wouldn't fit."

"Then take something out!"

"What can I take out? The freezer is full of green chile; what do you want me to do with it? Let it rot? Oh, everything is a mess, there's no room in the freezer for ice, all there is is chile and more chile and some old, what is this, meat? Is this meat in here, it looks old."

"Let me see, it's ham."

"Ham? This is ham? Where'd we get it, Mother?"

"Regino's compadre works at the packing plant, he got us the ham."

"There's no room for ice!"

"Put some cold water in the refrigerator."

"I did and then somebody drank from the bottle and left the cap unscrewed and then scooped watermelon from the middle, dripping seeds and juice all over the icebox and into the water that was in the bottle."

"It's *not* an icebox," Mercy yelled from the living room, where she sat reading *Ozma from Oz*. "*When* are you going to stop saying icebox? It's 1962, Rocío!"

"I can say icebox if I want to, Mercy; who's talking to you

anyway? Just shut up in there."

"Don't say shut up to your sister, Rocío. In my house you
will not say shut up . . . it's vulgar. You will *not* say shut up
to your sister, or to anyone else! Do you understand me?"

"Mother! It's just a way of expressing . . . oh, what's the
use? *Everything* is wrong! Everything! I hate this house, it's
so junky and messy and crammed full of crap . . . look at
this freezer, you can't even put in a tray of ice. We *never* have
ice; when people come over, we have to give them lukewarm
water from the tap . . ."

"It's good water, not as good as Texas water, but good."

"That's not what I'm talking about. *This* is what I'm talking about, this mess, this house, all of it jam-packed with
crap. I hate this house, you can never find anything, there's so
many newspapers and magazines and things! Let me clean it
up, throw things away. You can't even get through the back
room anymore. The last time I went up to the attic I thought
I'd suffocate. It's crowded and dusty and dark, and . . . I
wish this house would burn down! I just wish it would burn
down so we could start all over again! We'd get rid of . . ."

"Rocío! Don't say that! You don't mean that! It's our house
and it will not burn down, I tell you, it won't burn down, and
don't you curse it! I love this house, your daddy built this
house, you were born here, and we've lived here ever since,
this house is fifteen years old and it's full of *us*, our
things . . . you will not curse my house!"

"I am not cursing! Have I cursed? You don't know what
cursing is. All I'm talking about is . . . will you listen to
me?"

"I don't want to talk . . ."

"Then listen to me, Mother, will you just *listen*? I'm talk-
ing about this junk; it's a fire hazard. We could go up in
flames, but no, we have to keep the old newspapers and the
*Reader's Digest*s and the *Life* magazines . . . we have to!
That's what I'm talking about! That's what I'm talking about.
This."

"Someday they'll be valuable, Rocío! I like to look at them.
Sometimes I just go to the back room and look through old

magazines. I found a picture of Lindbergh and his family!"

"Mother! Let me clean it up, I'll save the important things, it's too crowded, there's no space. I can't find anything more."

"No. And that's final."

"Oh God. Well then, has anyone seen my book? I lost it again!"

"What book?" Mercy yelled from the living room.

"Don't yell," Mother said softly. "And don't curse. You will not curse in this house!"

"God, my book, the one I've been reading for weeks. *Gone With The Wind.*"

"You're still reading that," Mercy said, coming into the kitchen and sitting on the blue linoleum counter. She took a banana from the metal lazy susan. "I read it already."

"You did, Mercy?" Mother said incredulously. "When?"

"Oh, before."

"Where's my book?"

"Why don't you clean house today?" Mother answered.

"Mother! I can clean house any day. It's summer! Who wants to clean house?"

"If you're so interested in throwing out things, clean the house, maybe you can find something to throw out."

"Someone has taken my book again! And it was the same person that dripped watermelon seeds in the icebox."

"Refrigerator!"

"Shut up!"

"God, it was disgusting!"

"It wasn't me," said Mercy.

"Where's my book?" I demanded.

"I don't know."

"Are you almost done?" said Mercy, munching the banana.

"No, I'm not almost done; who asked you to come in here and join the conversation? You stole my book, Mercy!"

"It's in Mother's closet, I saw it there, Rocío."

"Mother! Did you take my book?"

"No, yes. Yes, I took your book. Ever since you started reading that book, you've done nothing around the house, nothing! Look at mi compadre out there, sweating. Why don't you clean house, work on the yard, *do* something!"

"It's summer!"

"And not only that, do you think you should be reading *that* book?"

"*Gone With the Wind*? What do you mean? Mercy read it already."

"Shouldn't you be reading something else, Rocío?"

"*Goona from Oz*, maybe?"

"*Ozma*, and it's good."

"Oh, go away!"

"Don't you tell anyone to go away, Rocío, this is *my* house and you will not tell anyone to go away, *ever!*"

"I'm tired."

"Yes, you should be tired, you got up at noon!"

"It's summer!"

"It's not normal to be sleeping all day. If you were a diabetic, I could understand. If you were old I could understand. If you were your father, I could understand."

"Please, Mother!"

"Okay, okay!"

"Can't we just throw away the newspapers and magazines, is that too much to ask?"

"Who is that outside?" Mercy said, staring out the kitchen window, leaning over the cactus and pricking herself. "Ouch!"

"Compadre Regino."

"Oh, what's he doing?"

"Pulling weeds."

"Ugh."

"God! He's got a job there, no way in the world I . . ."

"I will not have you . . ."

"Mother, please!"

". . . say God like that in *my* house!"

"He's pulling the weeds all right; it looks a lot better!"

"It does," said Mother, startled from her fury. "Yes, it

does! Ooooh, compadre, ¿cómo le va? ¡Oooooohhh!"
Mother said, leaning toward the open window and screeching
in an unnaturally expansive voice. "¿No quiere un vaso de
agua o una limonada?"

"What's he saying, Rocío?"

"I can't hear from here."

"So go look, dummy!"

"Don't you call your sister a dummy, María Merced!"

"He's nodding yes. To what?"

"Limonada?"

"¿Agua?"

"¿Agua? ¡Agua! ¡Allí voy!"

Mother waved to compadre Regino as he stood in the hot
July afternoon sun chopping weeds in our weather-beaten
backyard. The dark red and black fence was down, having
fallen over after an illegal garbage fire that spread to the rest
of the yard. It hung like so many charred and broken match-
sticks. Beside the fence stood a dried row of fruit trees: a lone
cherry whose only fruit that year had been devoured selfishly
by Mercy, two listless peach trees, the larger distinguished by
its singularly splayed, dessicated branches, the other shorter,
no less dry. Regino Suárez, the neighborhood handyman, had
dug trenches leading from one tree to another, to save on water.
They served as an artery of life to this phantasmic other-world
garden of Eden falling on hard times. The trenches were deep,
furrowing the ground mercilessly. They added a ravaged, bombed
look to what little yard of grass there was. How I hated this elementary, ditchlike series of veins scratched out of dried earth.

Regino was scything large wheat-like weeds near the basketball backboard. Near him stood a twisted, sadly-leaning
apple tree that never had any hope of growing straight or tall.
Nevertheless, the tree grew luxuriously. It was the only tree in
the backyard to still possess a will to live, the strength to try.
The tree was propped up by a splintered and decaying two-by-
four. Its branches sheltered and shaded of network of ditches
that all but ruined whatever basketball playing space was
available. These ditches had always caused us to stumble and
fall as we bounded the ball toward the goal. The goal was low,

not regulation height. Girl's height.

Regino stood under the basketball hoop, then moved the leathery, green hose over by the peach tree. The hot, flowing summer water cascaded from a small height into the round, weed-filled circumference of the tree's world, muddying the parched, much too tolerant earth that bubbled with lazy insects and small summer flies.

"¿Sí, comadre?" Regino said, looking up from his labor.

"¿No quiere un vaso de limonada, compadre?"

"¿Mande, comadre?" he said, a hand over his left ear. He was not a young man, already in his late fifties, his hearing not good, but, Bendito Sea Dios, that was all, that was all.

"Sí, comadre, cómo no."

"¿Limonada? ¿Agua?"

"Sí, comadre, lo que sea. ¡Gracias, gracias!"

Regino bent over and vigorously pulled an unusually large specimen of plant life from the ground. It looked prehistoric, invincible, other-worldly, the ancestress of countless weeds, accursed mother of our present shame. The rounded ball of roots struggled to hold on. Regino held the weed aloft like a trophy. This particular life was ended. He smiled to us as we peered from the kitchen windows, and then went back to work with the scythe.

Again, Regino swooped and struggled with the clinging vegetation, little by little swathing a path of his own—intent and not particularly effective.

Mercy sat on her perch by the radio; she flipped the dials back and forth, the screeching of voices and rhythms struck, now wounded the air, and hung there, suspended, full of furious impatient life. I looked out to Regino. "Turn that down, turn that down," Mother said, wincing. "How can you listen to that stuff?"

"What stuff?"

"Junk," she said. "Junk."

"I can't find the lemonade. Where is the lemonade?"

"Look there in the pantry, behind the clings."

"The clings?"

"Peaches."

"No stupid, next to that thing of mincemeat."

"Mincemeat?"

"Next to the hominy!"

"I can't see it! Where?"

"There, there!"

"Oh, I forgot, there is no lemonade," Mercy said, without any trace of emotion, "I finished it."

"God, Mercy, I've been looking in this stupid cabinet."

"It is *not* stupid, how many times do I have to tell you."

"You could at least tell a person! This is what I mean, the mess! There's no lemonade, there never *was* any lemonade, and there's no ice, and the water is hot and full of watermelon seeds, and oh, I just *hate* everything!"

"Just cool it, Rocío, okay?" Mercy said, going to the door. "Maybe Toncha can come over here for her hot water."

"Funny," I said, "funny!"

"Did Toncha call?"

"Oh yeah, she needs Regino."

"Why didn't you tell me, Rocío?"

"She called and I forgot."

"A long time ago?"

"Twenty minutes."

"Well, she'll just have to wait," Mother said. "At the moment, mi compadre is busy here. What's her problem?"

"Gabe," yelled Mercy.

"The water heater . . ."

"Tell your compadre . . ."

"Can't Mercy go and . . ."

"All you do is complain," Mother whispered to herself, then louder, "Take this water to Regino."

As long as I'd known Regino Suárez, he'd been the neighborhood handyman. He did all the work the husbands never did, never could. There was always a running battle to see who would secure his services first. Even this morning Toncha Canales had called to borrow Regino to fix her water heater.

"Water heater? It's already too hot, Toncha," I thought to

myself.

"You tell Regino to drop by on his way home, will you, Rocío? For some reason your mother thinks he's her personal servant. Now goodbye."

"By the way, how's Gabe?"

"Gabe," she snorted, "Gabe is Gabe. And how's your daddy? What have you heard from him?"

"My Dad? Oh, not much. How's Dollie?" I said haltingly.

"Dollie," Toncha muttered, "Dollie is okay. How's your Mamá?"

"She's okay and Mercy's okay. And Ronelia, well, she's got her kids."

"Well, since everybody's okay, goodbye. Tell Regino I need some hot water! Today's my laundry day and he's neglecting this part of the street."

"So okay and goodbye!"

"Who was that?" Mercy had called out.

"None of your beeswax. It was Toncha; she wants Regino to go over. Her water's out."

"So *you* tell him . . ."

"I *will*, creep. How's *Goona*?"

"*Ozma* and don't bother me. I'm reading."

"You're the one who talked to me!"

"I'm reading, okay?"

And so the morning went, Mercy reading, me looking for my book and Regino pulling weeds.

"You take this water to Regino."

"Mother, there's no ice,I've been trying to tell you, there's no ice!"

"So, the water from the tap is cold."

"Not *that* cold."

"It's not cold, it's hot."

"Just take this water to Regino." From the cabinet Mother had taken the red, metal glass, our oldest. She poured tap water into it.

"Maybe we should get a cooler," Mercy said.

"Someday," Mother pondered, "someday, when your

father . . . when we . . . go on, Rocío, take the water to mi compadre. It's so hot out there."

"Can Mercy . . ."

"No, now go and take it."

"Oh God, oh God, why do I always have to run these errands?"

"Now that's enough out of you, Rocío. That's enough. I never use the word, you know I never use the word, but shut up. Shut up!"

"Okay, okay, I'll take the water."

"SHUT UP!"

"Just listen to me, Mother, you never listen."

"You know me, Rocío, I only say things once. And that's that. YA."

"Okay! Okay, so I'm going outside to take Regino his water and tell him about Toncha."

"You tell him when he finishes. When he finishes to go to Toncha's."

"Okay, okay."

"Don't spill the water! *Where* are you going, Rocío?"

"Out the front door. I'm going out the front door. Is it okay?"

"Rocío, *what is wrong with you*?"

I held the red, metal glass. Too many flies. Why wasn't the house cool? Why did someone always leave the door open? I felt the heat, saw the faraway street leading where? To town. My eyes slid from window to window, the highest, the middle, the lowest. I could see someone outside, passing our house. He couldn't see me but I could see him. I imagined someone coming up the winding sidewalk, an S-shaped dream, a man, and watch it, Rocío! The water was spilling! Someone in a crowded car passed slowly down the street. I stood there with the red glass full of water, staring at the car. I was wearing my squash dress, dark green and navy blue, little squash-like patterns on the bodice and down the skirt. It was my favorite dress. It fit me well. As I stepped into the blinding midday sun, the red, metal glass grew heavier. I saw Ronald in the car, him of all people, and imagined him talking to Yolanda. Ronald with his greased ducktail and tight, black pants, his thick lips, vacant eyes. Ronald passed a dirty picture at the back of Miss Moran's home room, while Raymond Ontiveros pulled on Joanna's bra, pop it went and the dirty picture, really the negative of a woman in a brassiere, her flesh dark, anonymous, in luminiscent underwear, fell to the scuffled floor. I stared at Ronald as he passed in the slow moving car. Red sun, red glass, me in the dark squash dress. It fit me so well. Dark, lush girl in the sunshine, wanting shade.

Oh, and now I felt dirty, full of pictures. I drank the water thoughtlessly. I stood in the front yard. No one passed. I hurried to fill up the glass with hot, dense, clogged water from the outside faucet. It was too hot. I went around the house by the alleyway, afraid of spilling, to Regino. He had his back to me as he pulled weeds in the farthest corner of the yard. From where I stood, I felt his sweat. He was a small, tight man with dark, lush skin like polished cottonwood. He had no wrinkles and all his teeth. He was born in México, but as long as I've known him, he'd lived in town. I couldn't remember when I first saw him, I just remembered him doing things for us: fixing our pipes, unclogging our toilets, laying the blue Mexican tiles in the bathroom, body angled, crumpled, twisted, bent or flat, stick or tape or fuse in hand, silent, industrious, easing himself past us with incredible delicacy, knocking first, excusing himself, cleaning up quietly, and standing all ways, always above us on the blue, plastic-covered step ladder from the utility room, straining toward the ceiling, the stars. Compadre Regino never completed the sixth grade and yet he measured, tabulated, designed and ordered parts at the hardware store around the corner with its sun bleached, stuffed bear snarling in the window, someone's testimonial to manhood, bravery.

From the bottom of the stepladder I remembered Regino's dark armpits in his loose, white sleeves. I recalled the hardware bear, positioned so fiercely in the sun, his reddish-black fur a fading but still powerful vision at the entryway to the hardware store: a place of gadgets, nails, rods and tape, a place dark and full of mysteries—men's things, Regino alone knowing their secrets.

It was Regino who hooked up our faulty lights and tapped the circuit breaker, teaching us in silence the eccentricities of the television and the misbehaving vacuum cleaner. It was Regino who hand carried the second-party checks and who discussed in reverential tones the best, the least expensive way.

When Regino was needed, he appeared. He was the only one who ever emerged from the darkness to fill my father's place. He would appear in a dilapidated 1953 Chevy that was usually driven by his wife, the indefatigable Braulia Suárez. Seated next to her was her retarded daughter, Obelia, who was fat like her mother, with a wide-eyed, fatuous expression of oiled complacency without concern. Pressed to the front door sat the small compact and trim body of Regino, handsomely greying, with a benevolent expression of acceptance for this carload of his beloved obese.

Thus he would calmy arrive to help us, his other family. The back seat was always crammed with three or four daughters, filled with the likes of Lorencita, Dora, Arcy, Marquita or Atocha. All of them had large, expectant, bovine bodies that pressed together in an indistinguishable clump in the Chevy's back seat. As seen from sidewalk level, they were a wall of grinning, ever-growing woman flesh. Regino would emerge from the front seat, his space immediately consumed by one or another of the back seat daughters. Obelia would then stretch out like a purring cat, siding up to her mother's form with a child-like naturalness that belied her age and girth. Braulia would pat her, gun the floorboard and peel out down the small street, u-turning midway in front of a passing car. The herd of girls in the back and front seats were heavy-breasted, thick-thighed and unconcerned, indolent as well, and accustomed to full, hot meals and the fruits of their thin, wiry father's labor.

I felt Regino's sweat and approached, quietly, as he might himself.

"Regino, I brought you some water."

"Ah!" He dropped the hoe, looked down to the grass, wiped his face with a faded, greyed handkerchief, straightened up, came closer and apologetically took the water.

"Gracias," he said, in a low voice. Regino drank the lukewarm water thirstily, as if it were a golden nectar of life-giving elixir, handed the red glass back to me, nodded gratefully and returned to his hoe.

"De nada."

I walked quickly away. The water beaded on the rim of the glass; I could feel the wetness on the base, the gritty, sandy imprint of dusty fingers on the metal. It was a hot day, a long-drawn-out-shade-seeking-summer day.

I wondered if the door was still open. When I got inside would there be shade? The squash dress was too hot in the glaring sun. It stuck to me, my thighs, my legs, my breasts. The moisture pulled the dress to me. I resolved to find that book. To find it, lie in the darkness and read, read, read in the darkness.

Crossing the front yard, I sidestepped the dried, dying Willow Tree, I called at the locked door, "Mercy, Mercy, Mercy, open the door!" as the green Chevy drove up. The squash dress stuck to me in the sunlight. The car was driven by Eleiterio, Regino's only son. Handsome, handsome young man, with Regino's dark skin and bright eyes, he was the embodiment of whatever passion there was in the union between Braulia and Regino.

Eleiterio had come to take his father home for lunch. I banged on the door, "Mercy!" Eleiterio crossed the yard, silent, dark-eyed, knowing not to speak to me. "Mercy!"

At that moment a cloud of summer spray turned the street. An epidemic of encephalitis prevailed and the streets had been turned into a war camp by the city fathers. A heavy wave of numbing spray moved closer as the spray truck drove up. "Let me in! Let me in the house!" Fear and dread and wild fantastic exultation overcame me in the face of the moving grey wall. "Mercy!" I yelled. "Let me in!"

Eleiterio disappeared into the backyard. The door opened and I raced inside, sealing off the sun. I sank into the grateful semi-dark coolness of the quiet house. Mercy was stretched on the couch reading wonders. Mother was in the back room, attending to her documentations of the past. I stared out the highest window as Regino climbed into the crowded car. Eleiterio was at the wheel. The bright July sun was a reflecting prism down the S-shaped walk. Whatever passion there was, was mirrored in Eleiterio's deep, cool darkness.

The green Chevy disappeared down the small, hot, heat-waved street, toward the mountains. The sound of a faulty engine broke the torpid almost indissoluble silence of the beaded, sweat-stained afternoon. I peered from the fingerprinted glass of the highest window. I was enveloped and framed in wood. The outside shadow-crossed lawn was bordered by heat-seared, anxious red flowers, the zinnias that my mother loved.

I thought of the hardware bear. The heat. I felt the wet metal gladness of shade. "De nada. De nada. De nada," I said. And Mercy, "What, what?"

II

Regino Suárez and his family lived near the old viaduct, atop a small hill that overlooked part of Main Street, a site that in later years became the Police Department Complex. But in the fall of that particular year, Regino's house faced out catty-corner to Algodones Street, that farther south led into that part of town called Little Oklahoma, by certain particular and vociferous local residents who deemed the viaduct area little more than a strip of run-down, second hand stores, flea markets and small motels of dubious reputation. Interspersed here and there was a drive-in bar, a locksmith shop, or a greasy barbecue restaurant run by former residents of the old south who had migrated closer to the sun. This new tarnished south, in the minds of the citizenry meant gaunt, harried women with crying, mucous-crusted children and burly, monosyllabic men who had formerly worked on oil rigs and now drove trucks. East and west were the boundaries of the town, the farms of chile and cotton; east and west were intimations of space and proof of relatives who still clung to the land, and who were revered by the landlocked majority as part of a dying past. North was a point beyond knowing; it led to large cities, other cultures, a difference in climate. North led to mountains of snow, the organic process taken to its ultimate disclosure, the beginnings of icy cold rivers, streams and lakes whose water later became the crops of farms: cotton, red chile and green, beans and melons, alfalfa and onions, feeding man and animal alike.

In this valley, the high cold stony peaks seemed far away, as clouds do, bringing rain.

The Northern Road led to mountains and snow and cold, to government, and the removed arias of art and politics, to its aging, fading movie stars, to their summer ranches, and to my father, who had left his south for the crowded freedom of the north. Like so many people before him, he crowded ever closer to fulfill the unspoken law of northern climes: the closer physical proximity without the warmth.

The north my father chose was a world removed from the arid tension of the desert's balance. This northern world was removed from the hot, energetic cries of locust and coyote, from days of stormy wonder and wind. It was a world untransformed by the slow, impatient, hot, restless nights of incredible stillness, within which a great passion moved and breathed. The southern nights were nights of waiting, nights worth waiting for. Nights that heralded bright dawns in which dreams were heard, seen in the first glimmer of the daytime's moon.

Regino Suárez lived on the north side of town, clearly within view of the daily machinations of a growing city. The small hill on which he lived was nearly leveled, each succeeding generation having contributed to the land's patterning. It was a flat, open town, with great vast lots full of grey and pale yellow grass, and listless, half-dead mesquite bushes. Many of the lots were litter-filled with tumbleweeds, that, having blown to rest in March, still found themselves lingering in mid-October.

"*This* is what I don't like about New Mexico!" someone told my mother one day. This tourist was a neophyte to the desert, unused to the land, not burnt to recognition yet, not quite seeing past the scrub brush or the random and disquieting disorder. "This is what I don't like," she said, pointing to one of the many weed-filled lots around the city. "It's so *messy*, why doesn't *someone* clean it up. You would *never* find this back East!"

And in the midst of such a lot, now tamed, on a small, still distinct rise, facing Main Street, stood the Suárez home. The lawn was centered by a homemade cement fountain, inset with bright, twinkling glass, shards of pottery and colored bottles. Around the spacious yard ran chickens and several dogs. Fluted metal edging framed trees and a small, green yard to the side of the house where several bright blue, metal lawn chairs were positioned in front of a tiled table, redesigned from a former cable spool.

As seen from the street, the Suárez home was large, substantial. Set away from the street—framed, as it were, by the wild, uncultivated land—the home was an island of labor and order and will. Regino had an eye for the smallest of details, and his home reflected and articulated beauty.

Farther north and east lay Chiva Town, where goats and pigs once roamed freely along with fowl and other domesticated animals among the brush and the desert grass. Chiva Town consisted of several dirt streets, crisscrossed by countless smaller ones. Within the unregistered boundaries of this neighborhood lived a portion of the town's poorest families. Farther north and near the city park lay another world, that of the Fullerton's and the Brown's, black families whose sons either excelled in sports and were always winning scholarships to the state university or who were constantly in trouble with the police. So, on driving north and east from the Suárez home, one passed through parallel but disunited worlds, worlds surrounded by invisible yet real membranes that pulled and yielded and fell back once more into themselves—separate, distinct, part of the greater whole, and yet consciously marked off: Chiva Town and Brown City.

Regino's home was on the edge of Chiva Town, may one day have been in Chiva Town, but now the new elementary school and the resultant commercial development had forced the unspoken boundaries back, away from Main Street, away from Algodones Street. Regino's house was an island in the midst of the ever-expanding commercial sea and stood out in its unconcern for the flat, vast-creeping tide of dried, materialistic life that floated to the edges of what once had been hills, what once had been farms, what once had been.

And so, carrying yet another box of used clothing, damaged mechanical devices, scuffed, stained shoes and a full pound of yellow popcorn, we arrived on Suárez Hill. The wind was blowing softly, insistently, in that October way, a portent of a vague, stirring movement toward change. The trees, still covered with leaves, were listless, passing along responsibility to the other elements—the wind, now gaining, gaining, ascendent harbinger, mother movement of the dust-filled season. We arrived on Suárez Hill. Mercy was left behind.

Obelia sat in one of the dark blue, metal chairs, rocking back and forth and creaking with the backward push. Eeeeee. Across from her stood Zianna, the darkest, loveliest flower in the Suárez garden. A hose in hand, fingers laced over the hose head, Zianna watered the roses that grew near the street side of the house. She stood between the tame and the untamed worlds, that of her father's constant laborings and that of her mother's rampant, uncontrollable life.

Zianna's face, lovely as a dark brown, dusky rose, was lit with natural highlights. Her neck was long, her small, proud head balanced by a full, fleshed mouth. Her luminescent eyes shielded themselves against the elements and luxuriated in the absence of explanations.

Full, lush and firm, her breasts were carefully rounded swells of female flesh, flowerets full of awakening fragrance. Zianna stood straight, her face in the direction of her thirsty charges. Her feet were planted firmly on the grateful grass. It was late afternoon in early Autumn. The expectant air was punctuated by Obelia laughing to herself. Eeee!

The two of them were composite parts of their parents commingling life; one of them the dark, refined joyous consummation of ecstasy and the clear-sighted flesh, the other a clinging, wet, over-watered stalk of unseeing weed that perniciously attached itself to the elements. Feeling all the sun, all the moon, lazily partaking in the magnificence of animal life, Obelia was without the knowledge or concern for the subtlest, smallest glimmering *Something* out there, higher or more beautiful than herself.

La comadre Nieves drove up in her dark blue Ford, and called out, "Obelia, Obelia, ven acá." Obelia ran to comadre Nieves and tried to hug her through the small, half-rolled up car window. The noise of the rocking metal chair clanged in the air.

"¿No está mi comadre Braulia?" Nieves asked.

"Sí, Madrina, está en la casa."

"Let's just drop off the boxes and go home. We won't talk too long. Remember we're just dropping by, stopping off, no sense in staying too long."

But it was too late; Obelia ran behind la comadre Nieves, her large body swathed in polyester. The oversized white t-shirt bulged and strained with mistaken maternity. The mercury blue marks of the lawn chairs, accursedly famous for their colored slashes on clothes and flesh, criss-crossed her clothes. Still the chairs bled black-blue on the skin. The powdered paint was visible on Obelia's sausage legs and rolled fat-filled rump. Obelia, a merry, prancing pig woman, squealed "eee" and "ay" and "ah," and "Madrina, Madrina." Not *her* madrina, but Atocha's. Atocha and her sister piglet embraced *their* madrina, surrounding and all, but obscuring she who had come to reign/rain gifts on them. For Atocha there was a pair of white bobby socks, and for the other girls—Lorencita and Dora and Arcy and Marquita—scarves and handkerchiefs and faded sun hats. The summer was spent and all the offerings were dried out, heat-starched.

Obelia ran into the house with la comadre Nieves, who greeted all the girls by name. "Ay, Madrina, Madrina," Obelia squealed from behind the door, "¿qué me trajiste?"

"¡Sssstt! ¡Obelia! Déjale que descanse. Siéntese comadre, aquí en esta silla. ¿No quiere un vaso de Kool-Aid, comadre? Las muchachas lo acaban de hacer. ¿Qué le sirvo?"

"¿Comadre, no tiene una tortillita? Tengo ganas de probar de sus tortillitas tan sabrosas."

"Sí, comadre, con mucho gusto. Lorencita, trae unas tortillas para mi comadre Nieves. ¡Caliéntalas! Comadre, están retebuenas con mantequilla."

"Ay, comadre Braulia, no, fíjate que estoy en dieta. Gracias, Arcy, pero no quiero el Kool-Aid. ¿No me trae un vaso de agua, Dora?"

"Tráele un vaso de agua a mi comadre, Dora, por favor," Braulia commanded, pulling out a chair from the red dining set, given to her last year by comadre Nieves.

And so the boxes of clothes, socks, shoes, broken lamps and useless timepieces changed hands. "Las muchachas," all of them broad, hefty girls, quietly and quickly took the cardboard boxes to their rooms. The boxes disappeared into that inner sanctum, to be ogled over later in the high excited squawking that followed a visit of la comadre's. Visits from her meant a festive holiday spirit, a new dress, a pair of shoes, a plastic bag of circus peanuts or candied orange slices, and usually for Atocha, a small special token of her Madrina's love and constant devotion. There was always something for everyone, whether it was a pair of scissors or a small broken compact mirror, filmed over with too pale face powder, that nonetheless was interesting, for it *smelled* so good, reminding the girls of la comadre Nieves, her white smooth face, and her vast clean fragrant kindness.

Comadre Nieves' visits were regular, especially in the summertime when she was not teaching school, and had time to go through her things, sorting clothes and old sheets, washing them and making sure they were clean and mended. La comadre was not like other people; her clothes always came regularly and were always in the best of order. And she had good taste. La comadre Nieves liked pretty things, so her bags of clothes were of the best quality. Unfortunately, Rocío and Merced were toothpick thin and only Zianna could wear their clothes. But la comadre always had other things to make up for those dresses: hats, scarves, jewelry, shoes, elastic stockings. Let Zianna have the dresses! Dora and Arcy could fit into comadre Nieves' size sixteens and every now and then her sister in Texas sent her things. This Texas woman was the girls' sizes. So what if Zianna got all the Esquibel girls' dresses, what were they, anyway, but little dried sticks. And those Texas women knew how to dress!

But all this sorting out was done later, when la comadre and her daughters left the house. Usually the daughters were together, sometimes there was only one. They often stayed in the car, one of them reading in the back seat while the other sometimes came in the house and sat on the couch, looking quiet and staring at something on the other side of the room. They seemed in a hurry and were always anxious to leave.

"Marquita," said la comadre Nieves, eating her second to the last tortilla, "Go and tell Rocío to come inside the house, will you?"

"¿Otra tortilla, comadre?" dijo la comadre Braulia, her fat padded hand resting on the red, formica table top, the other busy with a dinner knife, unclogging the soiled grooves of the table's slats.

"You tell Rocío to come inside, Marquita, that la comadre has some tortillas."

Marquita passed through the crowded kitchen where las muchachas all sat around eating tortillas and jam. Arcy had taken out the margarine and Dora the Bama preserves and everyone was drinking black cherry Kool-Aid with ice.

Marquita passed through the living room and went outside, past Zianna, who was still watering. She heard the faraway mmm and then the deep body-gripping pull of the water churning from the faucet, reeling up and dancing into the hose from the bowels of the earth and then spilling over and onto the accepting ground, far away and somewhere behind the back of her head. Marquita knew the water hose was on.

She felt it in her body. She smelled the grass and what else would Zianna be doing at this time of day; wasn't watering her pastime, anyway?

Zianna would get her dress wet; she never wore pants like the other girls. She stood on the grass barefooted, with no shoes on and in a wet dress and never caught cold. She never did, she was never sick. But this time she might.

"Your mother says to come inside, Rocío."

"Oh."

"She's in the kitchen."

"Oh."

"Eating tortillas."

"Oh."

I said to myself: Now, go inside, Rocío. Roll up the car windows and lock the doors, you never know. Leave your book in the car this time. You'll go in and hurry Mother up, tell her, "Mother! Remember you said we wouldn't stay long." Go inside and tell her, "Remember!"

The day was still warm for October, even in the early night coming on time. The car's plastic seat covers were not sticking, the little, raised grooves were finally at rest, after a season of abrasion. I was sixteen, a junior in high school, and finally becoming someone. The enveloping stillness felt good. Allow yourself these lapses, Rocío. Why hurry? And on hurrying, where? For what? The car was a quiet blue friend, ready to take me anywhere I wanted to go: Main Street, Bob's Drive-In. I was looking for someone. Someone. That someone, Myself. A car full of giggling, smoking girls dragged Main and then went to Bob's for cherry cokes with lime. Later, cars full of boys passed. Once we saw Eleiterio. It *was* Eleiterio in the green Chevy! It *was* Eleiterio, whose father was so strict, who did not allow the girls to date. Compadre Regino was an Adventista. None of the girls was permitted to be seen with boys. Oh, they were content enough. On weekdays they went to school, except for Obelia, who stayed home. Saturday morning there were cartoons on television, and Sunday there was Church. It was all very ordered.

In-between were meals. The girls loved to eat. It seemed impossible to have seen Eleiterio in a passing car, alone at night, dragging Main, slowly, in that pseudo-pachuco pretend way, but he wasn't either a pachuco or dragging Main. I imagined things. Almost always imagined things, and only once or twice with Eleiterio. Su apá era adventista.

Ssssmmoosh. MMMMmmmmmm. Patter, patter, patter. Black bird, blackbird, *what are you thinking?* Zianna stood nearby, a part of the landscape. She was too wild for the garden's cultivation, yet too refined for the wildness of the Suárez home. She was a small, silent black bird on the nearest branch.

Ssssmooosh. Mmmmmmmm. Patter, patter, patter . . .

I imagined Zianna standing in the grass, watering, wearing the squash dress. That dress will be hers. Dark girl in the sunshine, seeking shade.

I saw in front of me our door. Our former door. The three Magi of perception peered at me with their panes—like notes, highest, middle, lowest. How many times I'd looked out to see the silent street, waited for cars to pass, and imagined faces out there in the darkness, coming to call for me. Our door now greeted me. Familiar friend with the knobbed eyelets, whose eyes stared into the days, hello! Wood of walnut gold and shiny still, hello. Hello my friend. My former friend. Having entered this house of would-be friends, you are the only one I remember. When did you disappear? The door that replaced you is now blue with intricately designed wooden blocks. Regino Suárez took the walnut door away. It was he who replaced it with another. He carried the trinity away to Suárez Hill, to the edge of Chiva Town. From this vantage point the praise continued, life went on, cattycornered, while las muchachas drank Kool-Aid and ate tortillas with margarine. They laughed and talked with comadre Nieves who knew them all by name. In the darkened living room I sat on the grey foam couch given to comadre Braulia by Toña Canales' sister-in-law, la Minnie.

The room was half-dark in the October light. The couch was soft, too soft. The tables and the television top and the counters were clean. The wooden tables nevertheless were dry, stripped of oil. Everything in the house was used, old, secondhand, mended, fixed up, someone else's, emptied of character. The only things that breathed some amount of fresh air were the plants, in coffee tins on a peeling green table by the window. They were comadre Braulia's babies. They were in need of water, transplanting. They lived, but half-heartedly.

"Did you call Rocío, Marquita?"

"She's in the front room."

"Rocío! Rocío! Are you there?"

"Prende la luz, Dora, está muy oscuro en la sala."

"Mother!"

"Come and eat some tortillas."

"Llévale una tortilla, Arcy, por favor."

"Sí, Mamá."

"You want tortilla?"

"Thank you."

"Come to the kitchen, Rocío."

"I'm okay!"

"Want some Kool-Aid?"

"I'm okay!"

"What's she doing?" la comadre Nieves asked Arcy when she returned to the kitchen for a glass.

"I don't know. Looking out the door," Arcy said, as she poured the drink into a red metal glass. "Eeeeeiiiii!" Obelia laughed, "EEeeee, el vaso, es el mismo color del Kool-Aid!"

"De veras, de veras, Obelia!" said her mother, la comadre Braulia, eating tortillas with preserves. "¿Pues comadre, no quiere algo más, un taquito de carne? ¿Unos frijolitos con chorizo?" asked la comadre Braulia, scratching her arm.

Mmm. Smoosh. Splash. Patter. Patter. Patter. The sound of water on the metal chairs. Zianna is still watering. Black bird, black bird, what are you thinking?

III

"Ay, se fue Regino, comadre Nieves. He left last week and he isn't coming back."

"And why didn't you tell me, comadre Braulia?"

"I didn't tell you because I kept thinking he'd come back. Every day I prayed. The girls kept asking about him and what could I say? Your daddy's left us, he's taken up with a chorreada on the other side of town. What could I say; Arcy's birthday came and went, and still no sign of her daddy. He's taken the car or I would have sent Eleiterio over there to the puta's house to bring him back. And then today he called and asked me to put his things together, and that he would pick them up later. 'Later? Later, when is later? You come home right now, Regino Suárez, you're a family man and your family needs you.' And he said, 'Vieja, I'm never coming back, except today to get my gloves that you gave me pa' Crismes and my warm socks.' 'And what about your calzoncillos,' I said, to which he answered: 'I have them on.' 'Well, that's good,' I thought, 'it *has* been cold, and no telling *what* sort of woman you've taken up with, it sounds as if her house is cold.' 'It is,' he said, half to himself, 'but let's not talk about it anymore, you just have my things ready. Tell the girls to pack everything up in the brown suitcase that I used to go to California with, to have it ready and waiting for me.' 'Regino,' I started to say. 'No,' he said, 'Now, goodbye.'

"Well, comadre, what could I say? The girls got his things together and were waiting in the living room, but he never came inside the house, he sat in the car and honked and Marquita and Dora went out and said, 'Papá, come in!' but he didn't. He drove away without wishing Arcy Feliz Cumpleaños, and she cried and cried, the poor girl. That night she didn't eat her supper and you know how she loves to eat, so I finally had to explain it to them. 'Something has happened to your daddy; he's out of his mind, but more than that, the Devil has power over him.' ¡Ay, Diosito!, I don't know any more, comadre, he's a changed man!"

"So when you called me this afternoon to find out if Regino could come and fix your t.v., I thought, I'll go over and talk to mi comadre, see if she can help. Maybe you could talk to Regino and tell him to come home, comadre, to give up that pelada, whoever she is. Now why don't you show me the t.v., and I'll see what I can do and then we can talk. What's wrong?"

"The horizontal isn't working. The people on the t.v. are all stretched out and every once in a while they get long and then sometimes there's two of them. One of them, not the real one, but the shadow one, is usually on the left side."

"That's it, comadre?"

"The real person is followed by this shadow person. It's usually worse at night, that's usually when the girls watch t.v. or me the news. How long have we had these shadows, Rocío?"

"At least a while. Two weeks, a month, I don't know," I said. "The shadows come on slowly, and now we get them all the time. The strange thing is that this shadow thing happens only on one channel. One channel and late at night."

"Just let me get in there and see. ¿No tiene un martillo, comadre? The last time I fixed my t.v. something like this happened, except the people were short and the picture was long and in the middle of the screen. We didn't have no shadows, though. There, that's it. Comadre, I used my knife. I fixed the knob for the adjustment, it was loose. There."

"The shadows?"

"Well, you'll just have to wait on the shadows and see if they come out tonight."

"Tell me about mi compadre."

"Ay, comadre, there's nothing to tell. He's gone. And now he's living with some desgraciada pintada chorreada and she isn't even young, comadre. I would have thought she'd be young, but no, she's not young and she's from our church! Ay, isn't that something! But anyway, she's a sin vergüenza and what does he care, puchee, as long as he has somebody to take care of him and wash his calzoncillos. What should we do, comadre Nieves, that's for you to tell me. All the time I fix t.v.'s; who says a man's the only one knows about how to do things? Ay, if there's one thing I've learned in all these years, comadre, it's to take something, look at it and fix it!"

Over La Abuelita hot chocolate and sugar cookies, las comadres decided that the thing to do was to go over to that woman's house and confront her. But not at night. In the daytime. That was best. That way no one could say anything against la comadre Nieves, la comadre Braulia or los padrinos or madrinas in their party, at the confrontation con esa sin vergüenza. Also, it would be less embarrassing if by any chance mi compadre was over there, God forbid, said comadre Braulia. Just as long as it was still light, because as soon as it got dark, mi compadre might be in bed in his calzoncillos, or getting ready for bed. "It could be embarrassing," comadre Braulia Suárez thought as she beat the dark rich chocolate cube with her spoon. "No, it wouldn't be good." No telling, no telling. She mashed the pure sweet candy-like chunks in the cup of warmed milk. No telling . . .

Later, on the way to la puta's in the car, Mercy and I could not believe that it was conceivably possible. Not Regino! Surely it's a mistake!

"Now, get in the car, I need witnesses," said Nieves, "We're just going to drive over there to Baca Street to la viuda Rael's, she . . . I need to talk to her about Regino. Oh, and we'll stop for Eleiterio."

"Eleiterio!" I said.

"Eleiterio—why Eleiterio?" Mercy rejoined.

"He's going with us."

"What for?"

"To help me find her place."

"Help you, what do you mean?" Mercy asked.

"Oh Mercy, to be there, in case . . . you know," Nieves said impatiently.

"Who is this woman?"

"A friend of mi compadre's, his . . . now, will you be quiet, girls!"

"His what?"

"Friend, friend. His friend. Now be still."

South from Suárez Hill, through the narrow streets of Chiva Town with its long rows of pink and green houses bordered by stuccoed terraces and metal grating from Juárez, was Baca Street and Mrs. Rael's house. It was a small, cute house with drawn curtains, a yardful of ceramic ducks and geese, a red windmill the size of a doll house, and bright red and blue planters with scalloped edges, like peeled away tin cans. And there were flowers, so many flowers, zinnias, lilies and large bushes of full-blossomed, moist-looking roses, not at all dried out as most of the town's, but soft-petaled, lush.

After a bit of a sisterly scuffle, Mercy planted herself by the driver's side of the back seat. I sat next to her, too close to her to be comfortable. On the opposite side in the back, near the door, looking anxious and compressed, sat Eleiterio Suárez.

The nights were getting colder and the plastic seats were brown and dry-looking, like the faded yellow fingers of old smokers or aged, careless diabetics. Between the seat and the seat covers were a few leaves, some dust. Only a short while ago it seemed the plastic seating had stuck to one's legs, leaving dotted imprints or hot slash marks on the backs of one's thighs. The seats had stuck to skin, sun and sweat mingling and leaving an odor of soft secret human places like armpits and upper arms. There was a faint aroma, a heavy sweetness like the odor of apricots or summer fruit.

The smell now in the back seat was of a male sweetness, the unconscious odor of a particularly aloof young man in the company of three women. Mercy clung to the door. I clung to Mercy. Eleiterio looked out the window, and in the front seat my mother prayed to herself that all would go well with the viuda whore, whoever she was. The Lord have mercy on her.

"Baca Street, Eleiterio?"

"815 Baca," he answered, in a short, clipped manner.

"815?"

"My dad drove me by there and showed me the house."

So! Eleiterio could speak. What he said was never of any importance. As a matter of fact, when given a moment of calm recollection, I never could remember the timbre or tone of his voice. When he spoke, all sound stopped and out of a vacuum I imagined sound and some sense of form. I heard his voice, but the hearing was nothing to be registered or even recalled, except with a disconcerting memory of absolute stillness. I do not remember Eleiterio's voice at all. No doubt it was quiet, with a certain halting inflection of someone not used to speaking. It was the voice of someone usually mute, stilled by a life in a house full of women, women and one other man. The only voice, the one true voice was Regino's, which was low, almost apologetic, but still straightforward. Matter-of-factly correct and polite and courteous with a touch of "Cómo está su Papá" and "Hello, how you been, what a pretty day!" There was never any need for Eleiterio to speak. Las muchachas could giggle, and they did, repeatedly and with great abandon, whenever possible, only to be quieted and momentarily controlled by a sideways "Ssssst!" from Braulia. For Eleiterio, there was never any need to speak, except to mumble an occasional yes or no in translation. I cannot remember Eleiterio's voice except as a large and empty and yet pronounced moment of utter silence within some sort of acquiescent murmuring. He had no need to speak.

In front of la puta's, Eleiterio sat in silence looking out the window. The sky was ocher-blue. The clouds formed a giant male with dark, staring eyes who was stretched out on his stomach with great elongated, flailing arms reaching out to a sea of vast approaching darkness. The cloud person lay on a deep blue raft, propelled through water, the small high crescent moon his only guide. La comadre's persistent knocking could be heard, then it stopped. The silence grew inside us as outside the crickets chirped and retraced melodies in their syncopated way. Ta ta ch ch ch. Nieves returned to the car. Mercy had opened the car door, rolled down the windows and taken off her sweater. "Why don't you get out Rocío; no, here she comes," she said.

Eleiterio looked away from the cloud man. "No one there," la comadre said. "She's not home." All of us remembered at once the Cinderella hour of our compadre's return.

"She doesn't have a car?" Eleiterio said from some faraway place.

"I'll come back later. Maybe tomorrow after school," said Nieves.

Nothing was said. No need. We drove away. As I turned back to see the rising moon, someone in the house turned back a yellow curtain. No need to speak. La puta was home, waiting for her man.

"Tell your Mamá we tried, Eleiterio, tell . . . you tell her we tried."

The night engulfed us in a wave of fine mist. Each day had its smells, each month, each year. Now it was apricots and roses. We heard crickets and a faraway yapping dog. And now another. They were talking to each other.

Who understands these words? The sounds words make. We felt the hardened, aging plastic creeping up in corners, cutting us. Our mouths were dry, our lips unmoving, as the darkened shore receded behind us. Baca Street passed by us, unlit in the narrow conduit of that flowered, trellised, sculptured world of Mrs. Rael's. What would she and Regino want from each other but the same order, the same clarity, the same beauty. Leave them alone, leave them alone, I thought. The town slept.

Why didn't everyone leave them alone. Meddling, the Christian way. But of course, it's understandable. There were the girls to feed, to clothe. There was la comadre Braulia, his wife—almost. After twenty five years of helping and doing things for Regino, a marriage license was of no value.

I should know, comadre Braulia thought to herself, I never got one. Enough you have a man, his children. What more? Let that puta desgraciada sin vergüenza chorreada vividora see if her flowers can hold him. The worst thing is that she's from the same church. So, after that, Comadre Nieves, I just stopped going to church, the girls too. All except Zianna, who sings in the choir. On Sundays I listen to Oral Roberts in English. So what if his son killed himself, the father is a good man. I sing all the hymns en español.

Jesucristo redentor
Jesucristo mi señor

Regino Suárez, por Dios, ¿qué te ha pasado, hombre? Like
I told Arcy, "Something terrible has happened to your Daddy.
He's not himself. He's a changed man."

Later, cuando regresó a la casa, I knew he would, I didn't
ask too many questions. Better to leave it alone. When something is wrong, you just can't pretend it's right. You can go so
long with closed eyes, but then one day you open them. If
something is broken, well you just have to fix it. And things
can't be fixed by doing what *you* want all the time. ¡No
Señor! Sometimes there's something that only *you* can do,
and sometimes there's *nothing* that you can do. And if you
don't do something when you can do it, that is, the right
thing, all sorts of horrible ugly things come your way. What
things? The wrong things. ¡Como con esa mujer! Well, she's
to be pitied after all. What good did all those flowers and that
cute house and all her plastic animals do her? What good was
the whole dirty thing, anyway, comadre? Regino already had
a family and she never could have one. La pobrecita got cancer of the female kind, so that goes to show you what's right
is right. Some things you can fix, some things you can't,
sometimes it's just too late. Now I don't know about that poor
woman, pero como le dije a Regino, "Viejo, if you get cancer, you can't say it was *my* fault!"

Ay, sometimes no matter how hard you try to fix things, you
can't. The Lord says, "Ay, so now what, do you imagine
you're God or something?"

That was all I said. It was enough. Basta. Se acabó."

IV

Nieves' fondest dreams include a fountain. Regino was
elected to the task, after her brief consultation with a few
other builders. "Why should I have someone else do it when I
can get Regino at half the cost, Rocío," Nieves said, "labor
and supplies included? Not only that, but he's a hard worker."

167

"When he gets down to work, he's on time. That's if Eleiterio or Braulia don't need the car."

"But he's mi compadre, Rocío," Nieves replied. "A compadre is a compadre. If I can help him in any way, I'm bound by the code. Then there's the added responsibility of serving as Atocha's madrina. Besides being Regino's child; she's actually more mine than his. Rocío, you don't understand. I'm bound by the higher laws of compadrazgo, having to do with the spiritual well-being and development of one of God's creatures. Compadrazgo puts me in a direct line to Heaven, that's if I respect the moral obligation of guiding the immortal soul of one of God's own. This means remembering Atocha's birthday, Christmas and other holy days of obligation. She was given to me as a gift. She's beholden to me as I am her.

"What if Braulia or Regino should die? Why, there's the madrina, that's me. What if Atocha were in trouble, God forbid, there's always a home, warm clothes, and food for her with me. God help a compadre or a comadre if they're lazy with their duties. Even worse, God help the ahijado, if he forgets who his madrina or padrino is. They're your one phone call and you'd better not forget that number, you remember that, Rocío. You could be left relationless, and what could be worse than that? You'd be disconnected from any living soul, unable to say 'tío, tía or hermano.'

"The warmth of a family is something you can't deny, but compadrazgo is different, Rocío. It allows the best of a family's qualities to shine through, yet there's a certain honest detachment. To be a compadre is to be unrelated and yet related, and yet willingly to allow the relationless relation absolute freedom within limits.

"Sometime, years before, even before you were born, Rocío, compadre Regino and I had agreed to become compadres. I had to think to myself:

1. Was I willing to hire mi compadre knowing full well the jobs could take six months, a year, be slipshod, and never to my satisfaction?
2. Was I willing to baptize Atocha, take care of her and see

if I couldn't get her a scholarship to the State University?

3. Was I willing to accept Regino's divergent religious beliefs and practices without a whimper, and still, in the bottom of my heart, pray for his immortal soul? You remember that shortly after the baptism mi compadre became an Adventista? O.K.

4. Was I willing to drive mi compadre anywhere, day or night, sickness or health, (my own or his) that of his family, without advance warning and at the last possible moment, without so much as a murmur?

5. Finally, throughout the years, was I willing to remain constant, true, unchanging in loyalties, and despite odd behavior, unusual circumstances and downright madness, still love, accept and *like* mi compadre?

"In summary, was I willing to accept compadrazgo—a union truer than family, higher than marriage, nearest of all relationships to the balanced, supportive, benevolent universal godhead? If so, I was a true comadre."

"Yes, yes, yes, yes. Yes. I said. And besides, mi compadre was a man. Tied to his maleness was the ability to do, to fix, to lift, to support and to think through. Now Rocío, wouldn't it be nice to have someone to *do* things around the house? When I was young that was all I wanted. Someone like my father. He was strong and he worked hard and he was there when something needed to be fixed. He didn't have any excuses. Never, not my father. Now Rocío, your father never could do things around the house, or if he could, he didn't want to. Oh, the first few years, maybe, when you were little girls and I said, 'Here, hold her,' and he would. And sometimes outside, he pulled weeds and threw them on the sidewalk where I'd find them. Well, that was something, anyway! But then, no more. And I kept saying to myself, wouldn't it be nice to have someone around to help *me*? Someone to do things? Around the house. If you get married, Rocío, find someone who will help you. It makes a difference. And it's hard when you love someone who doesn't care to help. It's very hard, a painful life, really, m'ijita. All the time wishing someone would help. It's almost too much."

"But, Mother," I said. "Regino never does a decent job. Everything always falls apart and he has to fix it again. Don't you get tired of driving him back and forth?"

"He needs the work, Rocío."

"I just don't understand. Why don't you get someone dependable? Regino's been digging in the yard on and off for two weeks and all we have is a yard full of trenches. It looks like we have gophers. It's embarrassing! It reminds me of the time when Regino put up the basketball goal. The same mess. The same slowness. The same methods. This fountain is going to take six months. We just finally got the tiles from Juárez, and that alone took a long time. Don't you think that someone else . . . ?"

"He needs the work, Rocío. It'll be a very pretty fountain. Just today mi compadre put in the water line. It leads from the side of the house near the willow tree, to the sidewalk. All you have to do is turn it on by the faucet. But now . . ." Nieves said, "Would you please clean up that toilet paper before anyone drives by. Who did that? Who wrapped toilet paper all over the rose bushes that way? Who?"

"I don't know."

"Who?"

"Someone. It's a joke."

"I wonder who did it?"

"Someone from the university?"

"I don't know. I guess someone wanted to play a joke."

"Get it all, Rocío!"

"¿Mande?"

"Clean it up! Oh, and don't forget to look at the fountain!"

The wind had been blowing for several weeks. Spring had auspicious beginnings: days of warmth, clear sunlit stillness. After a time of peace, the wind returned, a contrary, petulant personage. It was a wind that had crossed the sea, traveled over mountains and plains and found herself twining her soundless, undulating, pressing form between the budding trees and half-conscious shrubs of the new season. Spring struggled to come. Her puffing, gesticulating, incessant labor pains were intimations of a beauty yet to be born. The hard, green-brown limbs of the rose bushes were spiked and angry still. Now they were caught and twisted in the cheapest toilet paper. The paper ran around several times, then trailed to the ground and across the dry, earthsplit yard to the farthest bush, a cocoon-like larva. The tattered sheaves of two-ply fanned the air, the wind teasing them to a frenzy. On the opposite side of the yard near the driveway, Regino Suárez stood with his back to the street, shovel in hand, burrowing down to clear a path for the water line. He was nearly done with this part of the work, and he felt content. The work was going well.

I jumped over the sidewalk and began the process of stripping the bushes. The toilet paper stuck to the sharp thorns or floated away in the insistent, slightly chilled wind. When would summer come, I thought. When will we be done with this wind, this wind, this wind, that doesn't stop. A foot of filmy paper flew across the yard and into Regino's path. He picked it up and, dexterously moving through the broken ground, side stepped his way to me. He handed me the paper.

"The paper, it blowed to me."

"Thank you, Regino," I said, stuffing it in a paper-filled fist.

"I saw the paper and I said to myself: "Regino, what's this? Pretty funny, ¿que no?" He chuckled to himself, lifting off a few squares from the nearest branch. "It's the paper for the toilet."

"Yes, it's kinda silly."

"Pretty funny."

"Mamá was mad at *me*. I didn't do it!"

"El excusado," he said to himself, laughing shyly.

"Yes, it's pretty funny. Somebody did it as a joke."

"The college kids, eh?"

"Mamá wasn't happy."

"¡Ah, qué los chamacos!"

Regino peeled off another square of the paper and put it in his shirt pocket.

"¿Cómo está su apá?" he said, more seriously.

"Oh, he's okay."

"He's always the same, ah qué mi compadre. But he doesn't know what's good for him. Pobrecita, de mi comadre. Always waiting for him to come home. Ah qué mi compadre, he's lucky, if only he knew it. Your mamá, she's a good woman. Mi comadre loves the Lord, and He-loves her. He's the only one who's gonna bring your daddy back home. You take care of your mamá, Rocío, and the Lord'll take care of you. The Lord has taken care of me and I'm an old man. I'm not too old yet, but I'm getting older. And so is your mamá. You need some help with the paper?" he said.

"No, Regino, thank you."

"The work is good," he said, pointing to the dug-out yard, and the shiny new water line. "See, here's a drawing of the fountain; the water's going to come out of the top, and in the middle is this bath for the birds."

"It's very nice, Regino," I said, looking at a crude drawing. It showed a blue tiled bowl, from which a small spout emitted a high steady stream of water. The statue of Saint Francis would come later.

The tile was from Juárez, from La Casa de Oppenheimer. Before the fountain came the tiled basin in the bathroom. The fountain was an afterthought.

I stared at the creased, scuffy paper, the pencil markings detailing more than just a tiled fountain. Could I gauge that part of Regino that went into that beloved fountain of my mother's? It was a creative act of his, and yes, the fountain was lovely, for as long as it lasted. The water was the chief problem, either too much or too little water. The fountain switch sent up an enormous jet straight into the air. Two people were needed to monitor the fountain, one to turn the switch, the other to report on the fountain's height. The fountain, as a result, was rarely in use. It was a "company" fountain, a quiet, late-in-the-afternoon fountain. It had a pleasant tinkling sound and was loved by all the birds who bathed in it.

With a dark rush of softened wings, they flew away from that respite refreshed. From behind the door Nieves stood watching the birds bathe themselves in the late afternoon of a windy spring day. "Turn the fountain down," Nieves said, "Turn it down! And roll up the car windows."

Sometimes Nieves sat on the small concrete porch or on one of the metallic, blue lawn chairs and thought: How nice to have someone around. Someone to help me. Do things. All my life I've looked for someone. Well, it's quiet now, except for the crickets.

"Turn the fountain on. What, Rocío? Going out? Nooo-oo! Why don't you stay home? Higher. Turn it higher. Too high. Lower. Lowerrrr. . . . No, higher. And where are you going? Did you clean the kitchen? Are you coming home early? Rocío, just *who* spread that toilet paper? Was it someone you know? Leave it on now. I'm just going to sit here in the dark. I'm okay. We need a statue of Saint Francis. Higher. Put the plastic statue there in the middle. The birds, they like it. I just don't understand *who* would do such a thing. I came outside and my Saint Francis had on an orange life preserver. Why can't you stay home? Where are you going? M'ija, leave the fountain on and *don't* come in late. Who could it have been, Rocío? Who? Someone you know? No, that's too high. Lower. There. Now listen. Can you hear the birds?"

V

"Somebody's at the door, Mrs. Esquibel, there's someone at the door! Rocío, come and get it, damn it, stop ringing. What the hell?"

"What is it, Daddy?"

"Compadre Salvador!"

"How have you been, Regino?"

"Buenas tardes, compadre."

"Pásale, come on inside . . ."

"Nomás quiería preguntarle a mi comadre Nieves alguna cosita."

"Hot out there? Qué calor, ¿qué no?"

"You look good."

"I feel pretty good, Regino."

"Still living up North?"

"Yes."

"You look real good."

"I feel pretty good."

"Qué gusto verlo, compadre Salvador. Hace muchos años que . . ."

"Time sure flies, eh?"

"We're getting old, compadre."

"Not me, I feel good as ever. And you . . ."

"It's the Lord. He's given me good heath, a family, and all my teeth, compadre. Who needs anything else?"

"You want to talk to Nieves?"

"Sí, compadre, por favor."

"Nieves! Nieves! Rocío, call your mother. Rocío! God damn it, where are those women?"

"The Lord has sustained me, compadre. He's the only one. All these years of hard work and I'm still in good health. ¡Gracias a Dios! Oh, I got crazy once, compadre. It was Satan. He entered my heart. But no more. Since then I've been working for the Lord."

"Nieves! Damn it, where is she?"

"Did you call, Daddy? Oh. Buenas tardes, Regino."

"Buenas tardes. ¡Ay, qué muchacha tan bonita! She's a pretty girl, just like her mother. Sí, compadre, debiera estar muy orgulloso de las muchachas."

"Their mother's done a good job."

"Ay, mi comadre es una santa! She's a good woman, your mother, Merced."

"Rocío."

"Nieves! Regino's here! Damn it, where's your mother."

"She's in the backyard, watering."

"Watering, dammit, at this time of the day."

"I'll go and call her."

"Yes, she's a good girl. She's a teacher."

"Ah, qué bueno. Cómo me da gusto ver a una familia

junta, ¿Y el baby? ¿Se casó?"

"Did you say something, compadre?"

"¡Que Dios los bendiga, compadre! Y les guíe por esos caminos oscuros, que Dios los bendiga, compadre, y les proteja."

"Here she comes!"

"Usted se ve muy bien, compadre Salvador."

"I feel pretty good. No complaints, oh no, not Sal . . ."

"Ay, comadre . . . ¿cómo está?"

"Compadre Regino, siéntese."

"Comadre, ¿qué le pasó al water main?"

"¿Cuándo llegó, compadre? ¿Hace mucho tiempo? ¿Quién lo trajo?"

"Por chanza me dieron ride, comadre. Uno de los compadres."

"Dispense, pero voy afuera a ver al main. Comadre, con permiso. Compadre, con su permiso."

"Sure, you go right ahead, Regino."

"Excuse me. It's so good to see you all together. Your daddy says you're a teacher, Rocío, and the baby? What about your other sister?"

"Mercey's married and has two children. And Ronelia, she's got six."

"That's real good. Compadre, qué gusto. I'm so happy to see you again. The Lord bless you."

"Gracias, compadre."

"Come this way, compadre."

"Sí, comadre, ay voy."

Regino and Nieves exited outside. There was a silence and then a pause. "When did Regino become so religious, Rocío, what is he, a priest?" asked Salvador.

I could hear noises from the outside. A faraway bark and a high-pitched voice under the hum of a distant lawn nower.

"Christ, Rocío, did you see Regino's suit? Goddamn your mother; that's my old brown suit! She gave it to him! The last time I was here I brought some laundry, and after I got back home half of it was missing. She gave it to him, and not only that, but he was wearing my tie. Can you believe your mother? She'll strip you naked and give your clothes away to Regino Suárez and his family."

"*That* was your suit?"

"My old brown suit. I really liked it. It had a few years left."

We sat in the silence of a room full of marbled summer shadows of hair and arm and window frame. The air was hot and full of unvoiced exasperation. Our emotions were twisted, they whirled and danced in the unrelenting wind. Each of us felt alone, with the insidious seed of vague, unnameable discontent. We looked away from each other. Outside voices hummed, birds sang and the trees' shadows lengthened. It was five p.m. on a Sunday afternoon in July. Now and then, a firecracker went off, slicing the arid and empty air with token significance.

The wind rose.

"Christ, Rocío! Did you see Regino's suit? God damn your mother, that's my old brown suit! You can't bring anything into this house or it gets lost."

The wind subsided.

"You can't bring anything into this house. Last summer I left a box of shoes here and now they're lost."

"She probably gave them to Regino."

"I don't know. I still think someday I'll find them. Who knows when."

Nieves Esquibel entered from outside. She looked flushed, with the bottom half of her cheeks dotted with red.

"Nieves! Regino was wearing my old suit and my tie!"

"SSSshh! He'll hear you. I know it!"

"It was my favorite suit!"

"It was old and ugly. You of all people deserve nicer clothing. And the tie had cigarette burns and you told me you stopped . . ."

"*He's* wearing the tie, it's okay for him."

"I cleaned and sewed the clothes."

"The suit had a few years left."

"Mr. Esquibel, a man of your position deserves a better wardrobe."

"Mamá, by the way, did you ever find my shoes?"

"What shoes?"

"The ones I left here last summer, they were in a box, about six pairs of shoes."

"You never left any shoes here, Rocío."

"See what I mean? They're lost."

"What are you talking about, Rocío?"

"Don't be so touchy, Nieves. Your mother can never crack a smile."

"I'm not touchy. It's you who's touchy. You can't be here five minutes without blaming me for something."

"Christ!"

"No, you don't, you're not going to blame me or anyone for your foul mood."

"Foul mood. Damn it, I feel good!"

"See how he torments me."

"Oh, just stop it!"

"Not until he apologizes."

"For what?"

"See how he is."

"Christ, I knew I shouldn't have come. I don't care if it is July the fourth. Every time I come, it's the same thing, the same arguments."

"There you go again."

"I don't care."

"Don't you threaten me."

"I'm not threatening you, it's just that I didn't come back here to take your . . . your . . ."

"Mamá, please don't cry."

"I'm leaving tonight."

"See, see, always threatening."

"My head hurts."

"So does mine."

"You think it's so goddamn easy."

"Please, please."

"Oh stop crying, dammit!"

There was a small knock at the door. It was Regino. Salvador cleared his throat and Nieves wiped her eyes.

"Oh comadre, comadre . . ."

"Un momento, compadre."

"That's my goddamn suit, Nieves!"

"I know it! I know it! What do you want me to do?"

"That's my favorite goddamn suit!"

"You have so many suits, what's one old baggy, stained, beaten-up, ugly, brown suit? And besides, it was a winter suit."

"I wore that suit last summer."

"Please!"

"So why's he wearing it?"

"Sssh! He'll hear you!"

"I knew I shouldn't have come. Your mother gets this way every time I come here. That's why I don't come to visit more often. I'd like to come and visit, this *is* my home town; my mother and all my brothers and sisters live her, but Rocío, I just can't take it. You understand, don't you?"

"Mi compadre needs a ride, Rocío, why don't you take him in your car?"

"We'll take him; come on, Rocío, let's get some fresh air."

"Don't you want to eat supper, darling?"

"It's too early for supper. We're not hungry now. We'll eat later when we come back. Okay, Nieves?"

"Okay mamá, we'll be right back."

"Come back soon, I want to go to Morales Park and see the fireworks at eight o'clock."

"What? Fireworks? What fireworks?"

"Does Regino live in the same place, Nieves, over there by Algodones Street?"

"Oh no, he moved years ago. He lives close to the new junior high school, Piñones, over there by your uncle Lino's."

"Up there? When did he move up there?"

"Years ago."

"What's up there?"

"Houses."

"Houses, I know. What's up there that he lives up there?"

"Government houses. They're very nice."

"How long have the wetbacks been allowed up there on the hill?"

"He's not a wetback. If you'd come back more often to see your mother . . ."

"There you go again."

"Your Uncle Lino is very sick. He's dying. When was the last time you saw him? He always asks for you. On your way back you can stop and see him. Rocío knows where."

"Now just . . . Christ! Nieves, I'm just going with Rocío to take Regino. I don't want to see tío Lino today."

"He's dying. He'll die and then you'll be sorry."

"I know the way."

"You do?"

"Come right back; the park will get filled up and we have to eat!"

"So then how can we stop?"

"Just stop."

"Compadre, ¿ya está listo?"

"Sí comadre, gracias."

Later, on the way back from taking Regino home, Salvador asked, "Since when do the people on welfare live in two-story houses?"

"I don't know, Daddy."

"Christ! It's a mansion! It pays to be on welfare these days. How many kids he got?"

"I don't know."

"Regino Suárez lives in that two-story house and pays $25 a month rent, all utilities?"

"Seventy-five."

"How many kids he got?"

"Zianna, she married a soldier from the base and moved to Montana and the boy, Eleiterio got sent to Vietnam, and the others, they stay home."

"Christ, it pays to be on welfare."

"I was on welfare once."

"Christ, your mother never tells me anything. She's always quiet about things, so I have to ask *you*. Regino lives in that house? Hmmm . . . that big pretty house."

"It's very nice inside."

"He's still with the fat wife?"

"They got married."

"And the retarded girl?"

"She works at one of the high schools."

"It's hard to believe that those houses are low-rent, when there was nothing up there but dirt hills before."

"Uncle Lino's house?"

"No, I want to go home, I mean, to your mother's. Take a nap. And anyway, he depresses me."

"What about Morales Park? I was . . . going out . . . with a friend . . . I'll go and see tío Lino tomorrow when I feel better. The last time I saw him all he did was cry. Since when do the poor Mexicans live like kings in two-story houses; Christ, it's a mansion! Rocío, you take your mother to the park. It's July 4th, take her to the park."

"There'll be fireworks. Don't you want to go yourself?"

"I know, I know, but I'm tired. I can't be doing everything with her. We *are* divorced."

"It's July 4th!"

"Independence Day. You take her!"

"Why are you laughing?"

"Christ, it was my favorite suit!"

"That one?"

"Your mother, Rocío, she's a character!"

"Yes, I know."

"Where is it that tío Lino lives?"

"We passed it already."

"All he does is cry."

"Yeah."

"I'll go and see him tomorrow. ¡Ah, qué mi tío Lino! I never thought the day would come when that goddamn wetback would be living up there by my tío's in that mansion!"

"You don't want to go to the park?"

"Rocío, we'll go up there tomorrow, what do you say?"

"I'll think about it tomorrow."

"What did you say?"

"*Gone With the Wind.*"

"Oh. We'll go and pay him a visit. We'll go up there and pay him a visit. Christ, I never did think that Regino, up there, in that mansion, and tío Lino, dying. Did your mother say he was dying?"

"They're starting."

"What?"

"The fireworks."

"Since the morning, Rocío, it's that way, it's always that way. Baby, let me tell you, I'm never coming back. It's your mother, you know, she gets that way. Goddamn firecrackers."

VI

When it's autumn, it should be winter, and when it's winter, we wonder about spring. We think we remember time and the seasons. But we don't remember the temperature, the way the air moved, how the moon looked or how we carried our sorrows with us, bundled up in what passed for pleasures, activities, plans. The movement of time is such that memory allows us to forget. It was autumn, but winter was the true season. And in the brisk clarity of that shortened parade of dreams, winter held us close.

Regino stood to the side of the S-shaped walk which was now cracked and furrowed by grass. The lilies on either side of the walk were stunted, cut back, with dried, yellowed edges. The weeds jutted between the spent flowers and called attention to themselves. They were fierce, deep-rooted and simply refused to be vanquished.

"¡Hierbas, hierbas, hierbas!" Bend over, pull now, pull again and stop. Look around and wonder if mi comadre will take me home soon. If I had a car, I would go by myself. But to have a car you must have a family. And to have a family means to have people around to feed. To have a car is to worry. And I don't want to worry anymore. Let the Lord take care of everything. When Braulia and the girls left me, my heart was hard, a piece of rock that had lain in the sun too long. Yet there was a detachment. So when Braulia called to say, "Marquita's gotten pregnant and she wants to keep the baby and live at home, just like she always has," I said I'm faraway, I'm faraway soaring. Braulia couldn't understand that. And I thought, Braulia you too are soaring! You left me, you and the girls. And it's good. You've always been like black birds, cawing, cawing, and eating all the crumbs. Go on, fly! Fly! And then I thought: It was you, Braulia, who decided to move to Montana, to leave me here. Now Marquita is pregnant, Zianna is having trouble with her boss, and Eleiterio is breaking up with his wife, and into the drink, and go on, let him, I say! No one has a right to stop anyone from killing themselves if that's what they want to do. Nobody has a right to stop suffering if people want to suffer. Let him go through it, Braulia. Let him get low and then come crawling back into himself and the darkness within him like I did. Then maybe he'll be able to love. And you thought I was going to say live. What is living without love? Go on, let him. And when you go through so much, as I have, little things fall away, and if everyone were to leave you alone, in a place by yourself, like me, in my duplex, and you had no car to get anywhere, why there wouldn't be anywhere to go, or nobody to see unless you wanted to see them. And then all you had to do was look around and the Lord would show you things: places and people out there, and He would provide: food, friends, new slippers like the ones la comadre Nieves gave me for my saint's day, and a car, and if not a car, a ride. So, when Braulia said, "Don't you care?" I said yes and no. Yes and no. You understand me, don't you? Yes and no. No, I don't care anymore and yes, I care more than ever. But not about you, but about everything and everyone. Oh yes, I care! Somewhere far away and somewhere very close. And this comes through suffering, only through suffering. So leave the chamacos alone—let them figure it out, and oh, report to me, vieja. I still like to hear the stories. "You stubborn old man," she said "*you* couldn't come to Montana with your family, could you? You have to stay here!" No, I said, after all these years, this is my home. You don't understand, do you, vieja, what order is, and peace? Order is going home to my brown slippers with the wool inside, taking off my work boots, fixing a bit of food. Oh, I don't eat much any more, anyway. I wash my dish and my spoon and my fork. I drink my Sanka and then I go outside my duplex. It's really nice, vieja, it's by the new junior high school, one bedroom, a duplex, me dijeron, and it's paid for by the government.

Peace is sitting on the metal chair that I kept—I hope you didn't sell the others, vieja, and if you did, don't tell me. Peace is sitting out there watching the trees move and feeling the wind. And it's not feeling sad anymore, because you want people to be this or that way, and you want this or that thing and the flesh is okay but there's nothing, vieja, like the quiet afternoons when I sit in my chair. I look at the fountain. It's like that one I made for la comadre Nieves. I don't think about anything, vieja, not even the flesh. No, there's peace, peace and love. For no names and for nothing that costs anything. For nobody and nothing in particular. I look around me and I think of you. And you are part of this rainbow, vieja. In this dream of mine, I looked up and you were a light in the sky. A white rainbow. But then you said, "But a rainbow doesn't have white light, and besides, what a way to think of your wife! And I am your wife, because you finally married me, pendejo. Some husband you are! Okay, keep your white lights and don't move to Montana! Me, I want to see things, to live, and so do your children, they want to live too. Oh, they want a new life, a real life, they want and need the world. Ah, qué loco. A white rainbow in the sky, only *you* would say that, that's the way it is with you, loco!"

"That's the way it is," I said to her out there in the darkness. In front of my duplex.

Let them live!

Let them see the world!

Go on, fly!

You Braulia, up there in the sky!
You don't understand, do you?
And even that passed away.

¡Ay, estas hierbas malditas! Mi comadre will come and take me home. I'll come back tomorrow and finish the work. Maybe I can get some of the chamacos to come and help me pull these weeds. I guess I'm getting old. They need the money, esos chamacos flojos! They can come to la comadre's and I'll tell them what to do. Me, I don't need too much money now. Stop now and pull. Stop and look around. Rest. When I go home I can warm up that soup que me dio mi comadre Nieves y esas tortillas. I'll have my Sanka. I'll do the dishes and then I'll sit outside and watch the sky. Pull and stop. Pull and stop.

"Yes," I said, straightening up, "I'm getting old. I may be old, but I'm not a viejito. There *is* a difference."

Ay, I'll go home now. I'll come back tomorrow and finish estas hierbas malditas! I'll come back, you tell my comadre Nieves not to get anyone else. I'll come back and finish later . . . I'll come back . . . and finish . . . Later. ¿Bueno? Okay!

"What are you giving Regino for his birthday, mother?" I asked. We were in a car.

"A bathrobe, Rocío, to go with his slippers."

"The same one you gave Daddy."

"They were on sale and your Dad will never know."

"Does Regino wear them?"

"Yes, he wears the slippers."

"How is he, and where does he live?"

"Alone. Braulia and the girls moved to Montana to be close to Zianna and her husband. She married a soldier from the base."

"And Eleiterio?"

"I don't know, he got married, has a baby."

"But Regino . . ."

"They left him alone, his family left him alone."

"And isn't he lonely?"

"Yes, he was, but I said, 'Compadre, you're better off now. All you did was worry about the girls.' The girls wanted to date and he wouldn't let them. He was too strict. They moved away so they could date. Oh, they wanted him to go with them, but 'No', he said, 'this is my home.' "

"Isn't he lonely?"

"Yes. But later on, he said to me: 'You were right, comadre, the Lord has given me peace of mind, just like you with compadre Salvador. Praise God. Praise God.' "

"I don't know," I said, "it seems so hard, to have left him, that way, so hard."

"Oh, he's better off, but yes, it's hard, Rocío, it's very hard. It's hard for me, everyone gone. But I have peace of mind. I have peace of mind now. It's taken so long, so long."

"Just the same . . ."

"No, Regino's all right. Now, don't you worry about me. I'll be okay."

"How's your family?" I started to say to Regino the next time I saw him, but then I stopped. "How's your new place?"

It was late morning. Regino was out in the front yard pulling weeds. He looked the same, still handsome, still with a mouthful of teeth, but now he was stooped, slightly breathless.

"It's the heat," he said, trying to account for his tiredness. He stood solemnly, wiping a sweat-filled brow. "It's so hot."

"That never changes," I said, and looked away and then back.

"Your mamá," he said, "she's not so well, I had this dream. Rocío, all she needs is to have you girls come back home and she comes to life. She's always busy with things, but when you are here, she comes to life again. I had this dream, Rocío. I don't know, it's good to see her come to life again."

Regino propped his hand on the upraised hoe. "Ay, that's all for today."

VII

"Compadre, quiero presentarle a mi hermano, Roque, y a su hijo, Tommy," Nieves said. "This is my compadre, Regino Suárez, Roque. Pase pa' dentro, compadre. Roque quiere comprar unos tamales y le dije que usted tenía un compadre que hacía tamales en la fábrica, La Buena."

"Sí comadre, cómo que no. La comadre Nieves bautizó a mi hija, Atocha," he said to Roque.

Later Roque and Regino sat on the living room couch talking about the weather, tamales and the merits of California. One year Regino had picked fruit up by Bakersfield. "It was a happy time," he said wistfully, sitting on the edge of the dark blue sofa. Regino never sat back fully, he was always perched on the edge of the chair or couch, ready to jump up, spring forward, take off in any given direction. When I entered the room, freshly made up, dressed up in a white blouse and long cotton skirt, Regino rose.

"Rocío!"

"Tío Roque! Tommy! How are you and when did you get in?"

"A little while ago, chula."

"Buenos días, compadre."

"Dios la bendiga, Rocío. ¿Cómo está?"

"Muy bien, compadre. ¿Cómo está . . . el apartamento?"

Stop. Stop and pull. Now rest.

"Vamos a traer tamales. Rocito. Do you want to come with us, pretty girl?" Roque said.

"¿Adónde van, tío?"

"A La Buena."

"The tortilla factory?"

"To get tamales," said Tommy.

"They sell tamales? I didn't know that."

"Sí," said Regino. "Mi compadre Wenceslao los hace."

"They sell tamales?"

"Nieves, hermana, deja esas cosas, we're going for tamales."

"Can we all fit in the car, Papi?"

"Hell yes, Tommy!"

"Ah, qué Roque, fíjate, compadre, ¡Este panzón barbón es el baby! ¡Es el baby de la familia!"

"Eeeeh, qué baby tan feo!" Roque joked.

"Oh no, Señor Roque," insisted Regino.

"So let's go, Dad. You get in the back with mi tía Nieves and Rocío, and Regino and I will sit up front, para que me dirija, compadre."

"Oh, no," compadre Regino protested, "Yo me siento atrás."

"Compadre, siéntese adelante con m'ijo. Are we in? ¿Nalgas listas?"

"Can we all fit?" Nieves said, giggling like a schoolgirl. I sat in the middle, between the fat and aging joyful brother and sister.

"¡Es el baby, compadre Regino!" Nieves laughed.

"¡Ah, qué baby tan feo!" Roque protested.

"Mi baby acaba de graduar con su B.A.," Roque said.

"She's a pretty good student," said Tommy.

"¿Usted no tiene familia, compadre Suárez?" dijo tío Roque con mucho respeto.

"Now then, Roque was the baby, compadre," Nieves said, "then there was Alicia and Manuel. And the others. They're gone now. That's four of them. And Mom and Dad, all gone."

We drove down the familiar, once small, magical, east-facing street to La Buena and the tamales that would find their way to tío Roque's house in Ventura, to tío Roque's wife and his two educated children, one with a B.A. in Home Ec, the other with an M.A. in Business.

Goodbye to the street and hello to Chiva Town. La Buena Tortilla Factory.

"I'll go inside and talk to mi compadre," Regino said. "I'll get the tamales."

"Aquí tiene dinerito, compadre."

"I'll be right back."

"And so what do *you* do," Tommy asked, turning to me in

the back seat. "I hear you write."

"She's a famous writer," tío Roque said, as we waited for the tortillas. "Or she will be. Aren't you a writer, Rocío?"

"Yes," I said, "I write. I'm a writer."

"He was such a pretty baby, Rocío," Nieves said, patting her greyed brother's head. "So pretty, with bright, big eyes and huge, beautiful eyelashes. Everyone thought he was a girl."

"¡Ah, qué Nieves!"

"He was a pretty baby, Rocío, and now look at the canas!"

"No, Nievesita. I'm not a baby anymore. Tommy, you help compadre Regino with the tamales."

"¡Estoy bien! ¡Estoy bien! I can carry them."

"Regino's getting old, Rocío, have you noticed?"

"Yes, I have."

"His family lives in Montana," Nieves said to her brother.

"He just can't work as hard as he used to and tires easily. But I still give him jobs."

"The door, Mother," I said.

"What, Rocío, do you like it?"

"No, no," I thought, it's ugly and I don't want you to be afraid. If you are afraid, I will be too. Take off the metal bars and bring back the trinity.

"Donacio did the work."

"The screen door is coming apart and . . ."

"Oh, I know, I know, there's so much to do! Rocío, so much to do, and no one to help me. No one to do it. All I ever wanted was for someone to help me."

"When did you get the new door?"

"Oh, it's been a while, don't you like it?"

"¡Eh, Papi, están calientitos! ¡Pero de de veras!" shrieked Tommy.

"¡Tamales de La Buena! ¡Qué treat! ¡Los vamos a llevar a Califas, compadre!"

"¿Bakersfield?"

"Ventura, compadre. Ventura."

"¿Por dónde queda Ventura? ¿Está cerquita de Bakersfield?" Regino asked.

"Here, Tommy, let me hold them."

"I got them."

"Okay, writer, now hold these tamales."

"Did you fix the door?" I said to Regino earlier that morning, pointing to the dark metal grating that outlined the front door. It was clumsy work, and it clanged and banged each time someone opened or closed the door. The blue metal was oversized, ominous, repelling easy entry. It was the door to a fortress now, where inside Nieves locked herself in, afraid of strangers, herself a stranger. Afraid. All the windows, too, were covered with the dark blue iron which blocked the lingering view from the outside world.

"Oh no," he said, "your mother's other man, Donacio. He did it."

"Donacio?" I said, with surprise.

"He's a primo from Tejas."

Later we sat down to eat hot tamales. It was the first time Regino and I had sat down together at a table.

"Siéntese, compadre, vamos a probar los tamales. Echame unos calientitos, Tommy. From the bottom, son. Now pass the plate to compadre Regino. Now Nieves and the writer."

"¿No quiere algo de tomar, compadre?" I said. "¿Jugo? ¿Leche? ¿Agua?"

"He can't hear you. Speak louder," Nieves whispered.

"¿No quiere algo de tomar?"

"Louder."

"Just give him a glass of water, Rocío."

"Nomás un tamal, por favor. Gracias, comadre."

"Gracias a usted, compadre."

"No, no, es nada."

"He's ready to say grace, Rocío, wait."

"Divino Pastor, le doy gracias por este día de tantas bendiciones, por la comida, por el sol, por el trabajo y especialmente por el amor que se difusa y se ve en estas caras, las caras de tus hijos. Que aquí están celebrando los misterios de tu divina vida y muerte. Le damos gracias Señor Jesucristo, redentor y le pedimos que nos dé la fortaleza para que poda-

mos servirle con todos nuestros corazones, ahora y en adelante, Amén."

"¿Otro tamal, compadre?"

"¿Mande?"

"¿Echame otro, Tommy"

"So where's Mercy?" tío Roque asked, unshucking a
tamal.

"She lives up North. Me too. Somehow it just happened."

"I miss them, Roque. I miss my girls," Nieves said sadly.

"Mamás! They never give up, do they, Rocío?"

"No, I never will, Roque. Never. Someday my girls will
come home."

"¿Más jugo, compadre?"

"¡Qué tamales tan ricos!"

"They're pretty good!"

"It's a feast! And we still have some to take home to your
mother, Tommy."

"So what do you do, Rocío?" Roque said, "I mean, can
you make a living? What do you write?"

"Oh, about people. New Mexico. You know, everything."

"I tell her, Roque, to write just one *Gone With the Wind*. I
say, Rocío, just write about this little street of ours, it's only
one block long, but there's so many stories. Too many stories!
And then I thought to myself, but why write about this street?
Oh, there's Toncha and Gabe and Manuelita Acevedo at the
other end with her ugly little dog and across from her La
Prieta Armendáriz and her flowers. Oh, there's the stories all
right, but why write about this street? Why not just write
about 325? That's our house! Write about 325 and that will
take the rest of your life. Believe me, Rocío, *at least* the rest
of your life. Just write about this house: there's you and your
Daddy, que Dios lo cuide, and Mercy and her kids, and
Ronelia and her kids, and me, don't forget *me*! I could have
my own book! I tell her, Roque, just write one *Gone With the
Wind*. That's all. Just one. You don't have to go anywhere.
Not down the street. Not even out of this house. There's stories, plenty of them all around. What do you say, Rocío?"

"¿Más tamales, anybody?" I said. "¿Compadre?"